"Here it is, a message from Jim!" Roberta cried.

> ## DESPERATELY SEEKING SUSAN
> Keep the faith. Tuesday, 10:00 A.M.
> Battery Park. Gangway One. Love, Jim.

"Who's Jim?" Leslie asked.

"Oh God, Tuesday. That's tomorrow!"

"Who's Susan? You *know* these people?" Leslie pulled her head out from under the drier and peered at the newspaper.

"Jim follows Susan all over the country," Roberta explained. "Last January she was in Mexico City, then Seattle. They send messages back and forth through the personal columns in the paper. That's how they hook up. Now they're in New York."

She sagged back under the drier, smiling to herself. What must it be like to be a woman like Susan, so desired, so hunted?

Oh, Roberta Glass wished that once, just once . . .

"Desperate," she said. "God, I love that word. It's so romantic."

■   □   ■

Susan relaxed and read The Personals.

"Jimmy . . ." she whispered, for there it was, just what she had been waiting for. *Desperately seeking Susan,* it said. She laughed. Her heart actually flipped. She got all damp underneath her clothes.

"It's about time," she said to herself, drawing a valentine around The Personal with her black eyeliner.

A SANFORD-PILLSBURY PRODUCTION

A SUSAN SEIDELMAN FILM

DESPERATELY SEEKING SUSAN

STARRING

ROSANNA ARQUETTE

AIDAN QUINN

AND **MADONNA** AS SUSAN

WITH **ROBERT JOY**

EXECUTIVE PRODUCER MICHAEL PEYSER

WRITTEN BY LEORA BARISH

DIRECTED BY SUSAN SEIDELMAN

PRODUCED BY SARAH PILLSBURY AND MIDGE SANFORD

MUSIC BY THOMAS NEWMAN

DIRECTOR OF PHOTOGRAPHY ED LACHMAN

PRODUCTION DESIGNER SANTO LOQUASTO

An **ORION** PICTURES Release

DESPERATELY SEEKING SUSAN
The Novel

By Susan Dworkin
Based on a Screenplay by Leora Barish

Harmony Books/New York

Published by Harmony Books, a division of Crown Publishers,
Inc., One Park Avenue, New York, New York 10016 and
simultaneously in Canada by General Publishing Company
Limited

Harmony and colophon are trademarks of Crown Publishers,
Inc.

Manufactured in the United States of America

Library of Congress Cataloging-in-Publication Data

Dworkin, Susan.
    Desperately seeking Susan.

    I. Desperately seeking Susan.   II. Title.
PS3554.W87D47   1985   813'.54   85-16414
ISBN 0-517-55976-5

10 9 8 7 6 5 4 3 2 1

First Edition

DESPERATELY SEEKING SUSAN
The Novel

Nobody could figure out what to give Roberta Glass for her twenty-sixth birthday because Roberta Glass had everything.

She had a three-story town house across the Hudson from New York in Fort Lee, New Jersey. She had built-in sofas upholstered in the newest chintz, recessed lighting adjustable to four different intensities depending on your mood, a maroon BMW in the shop and a brand-new black Ford convertible with a perfectly adequate radio. However, Gary, Roberta's handsome husband, wanted the radio replaced by a new eight-speaker AM-FM receiver and Dolby XBD compact disc recorder with equalizing fast-forward/audio-reverse digital tuning, floor mounted.

"Why floor mounted?" Roberta asked Gary.

"Because great sound rises," Gary said.

Roberta also had a high-tech white-tile kitchen with

an oven-stuffer-roaster-size rotisserie, a coffee machine that ground the beans and perked the brew upon signals from a presettable electronic clock, a garbage compactor, a garbage disposal, a retractable rack on casters just for pot lids, and a great maid named Daisy. Also in this wonderful kitchen, Roberta had a counter-top computer programmed with recipes and menus for every conceivable occasion, including the favorite foods of her father and stepmother for when they visited from Florida and the soft, mushy stuff her beloved dog, Dorothy, had liked to eat during those difficult last days before the end.

Roberta had been in the habit of talking to Dorothy when she was puttering in her kitchen alone.

Now she sometimes talked to the computer.

Roberta's oven was attached to her VCR in such a way that she could tune in one of eighty-five Julia Child tapes whenever she wanted to cook something fancy. That was Roberta's big talent—fancy cooking. However, Gary's doctor said that Gary was getting too chubby from Roberta's great cooking, and, since Gary was a workaholic Type A personality, Gary had to go on a diet. No salt, no sugar, no cream, no liquor, no grease, no organs.

The diet was working.

After four years of marriage and enormous financial success, Gary Glass had started losing weight, and, in fact, his wife, Roberta, was now beginning to see less and less and less of him.

Roberta's wonderful house had three bathrooms. A brown-and-pink tile. A green-and-gold stone. And a white–egg-yolk marble with opaque glass doors leading outside to a personal-size swimming pool. This pool was flanked with pink geraniums and cabinets full of fine wine and adjustable chaises with attached brass racks for magazines and snacks. It had a ten-foot fence all around that bristled with ivy and chirping birds, and if they had wanted, Roberta Glass and her husband, Gary, could have gone swimming there stark naked at midnight in the summer without being seen by anyone else in Fort Lee.

But Gary preferred to swim laps in the morning. It was part of his health plan. By midnight he was usually fast asleep in their orthopedic built-in bed in the beautiful bedroom with the pink-ripple wallpaper and the matching pink-ripple drapes, or else he was out someplace with a client, making another lucrative deal.

On those nights, Roberta would sometimes swim by herself alone under the stars, just thinking. She wondered why, now that she was married and having more sex, she was enjoying it less. She wondered if maybe Gary had discovered something irritating about her body. Maybe her breasts were too large for her slender frame. Maybe her arms were too thin; she *did* have thin arms, and if she went to the gym with her sister-in-law and lifted weights, her arms just got thinner. Maybe her eyes were too far apart or her chin too chiseled; maybe she should have had her overbite corrected years ago; that was it, she would get braces; no, she wouldn't; well, maybe. . . . But then she thought she was being silly, that none of these things really constituted a reason for the turn her life was taking. She simply could not get her husband to look at her. He kissed her and told her about his business, but she had the feeling that he never really *looked* at her for all that. She felt that she was becoming invisible to him, and she was afraid that, if this kept up, she would soon be invisible to herself. Nothing made her feel really alive except reading The Personals in the New York *Mirror* and fantasizing about other people's fantasies.

Lonely widower, not yet old, needs help recovering after wife's illness and long-enforced celibacy. Only the patient and tender need apply.

How old is "not yet old"? Roberta thought. She imagined the gaunt wife, wasting in a great four-poster bed, the large, sad man hunched over her, serving soup. She imagined him walking slowly out of the funeral parlor, convinced he would never get hard again, when in fact there was patient, tender Roberta Glass stark naked in her personal pool right across the Hudson. Dare she respond to his ad? Of course she didn't dare. Roberta Glass never dared to do anything.

Please come home, Harry, said one passionate advertiser in The Personals, *I can't live without it. Your slave, Shirl.*

What could Harry possibly have that would cause a woman to debase herself so voluptuously in the public press? Roberta wished she knew where Shirl lived, so she could be there when Harry came home and Shirl came running out of the house, leaping on him, tearing at his clothes. . . . She tried to bring herself back to reality by steeping herself in sexual advice from popular psychologists; she read whole volumes about how you have to be sympathetic to the pressures on a regular guy like Gary when he is engaged in making a fortune. She tried keeping a diary. She tried to like her life, her abundant jewelry, and her walk-in closet full of designer clothes from Bendel's and Bergdorf's and boutiques on the Costa del Sol; she tried very hard to like herself. But in her diary, the only really interesting stuff concerned a guy named Jim who sent messages to a girl named Susan through a series of personals in the newspaper, which Roberta waited for avidly, with a thumping heart— just as her grandmother had awaited the next install- ment of some serialized novel and her stepmother waited for the next episode of her favorite soap. Compared to the high drama of the long-celibate widower, compared to the Technicolor passion Shirl had for Harry and Jim had for Susan, Roberta felt as faded as an old pastel. Twenty-six years old, she said to herself, only twenty-six and already fading.

She floated on her back, her shiny blonde hair drifting out around her face, her pretty pink toenails and her pretty pink nipples protruding out of the water, and she watched the George Washington Bridge dance on glittering ropes of rhinestone lights across the sky to New York City, and she dreamed of being in love.

The enormously successful business that kept Ro- berta Glass so happy and contented was Gary's Oasis, the largest collection of spas and hot tubs east of the Rocky Mountains. Whole families of shoppers from Manhattan and Queens, and as far away as Connect- icut and Westchester, would come to Gary's Oasis on day trips to wander among an endless array of bub- bling, spurting, swirling bath models in tile and Lu- cite, Plexiglas and redwood, marble and imitation sequoia, all assembled in a mammoth showroom in the shadow of the Meadowlands' Byrne Arena. Gary Glass's spas and hot tubs were so popular that he found he could barter them easily for other costly and desirable items. Like root-canal work. And cases of fine wine. Like the new eight-speaker stereo for the Ford that he was anticipating with keen delight. And the services of some of the most beautiful young TV actresses ever to be handled by Becky Shuman's chic agency.

Ordinarily, Becky Shuman would not have bothered with a retailer. A tall, dark, smart woman with a great lust for power, she usually did casting only for multinationals. But Gary Glass waltzed into her office with that cute grin, so boyish, and handed her into his company limousine and drove her out to Gary's Oasis, where she fell in love with a scarlet-marble hot tub that came with its own perfumed waterfall. In the middle of a business day, when Gary's Oasis was packed with spa seekers, Gary pulled a retailing unthinkable: He closed off the marble wing and let Becky Shuman, the casting director, bathe in private.

Jungle birds squawked. Fly-catching black orchids snapped up anything that buzzed. Luxuriating in her scarlet waterfall, Becky felt like Brooke Shields, but evil. The retailing unthinkable had done the trick. In exchange for having this great turn-on installed in her condo, Becky agreed to provide, gratis, the supporting cast of beauties for a TV commercial about Gary's Oasis, which starred none other than Gary Glass himself.

Gary and Becky had spent many pleasant days together while making this commercial. It was due to appear on television for the first time tonight, at

10:58, in the middle of Roberta Glass's twenty-sixth-birthday party.

Right before lunch on the day of his television debut, Gary's sister, Leslie, called.

"Did you buy Roberta a present?" she snapped.

"Oh my God, I forgot," said Gary.

"I knew you would forget. You're a pig, just like Daddy. Send your secretary to Cartier this instant."

Leslie hung up.

Gary buzzed his secretary.

"Get the limo, go to Cartier's, and buy my wife, Roberta, something for her birthday," Gary said.

"But what?" the secretary asked.

"I don't know, something, anything. I mean, she already has everything, so it doesn't matter, does it?"

"But how will I know what she likes?" the secretary asked.

"Don't worry about it," Gary answered. "Roberta's very easily satisfied."

The secretary took off for New York, with a blank check. Gary leaned back in his executive swing chair. He lit a large Cuban cigar. He was feeling great. Already this morning he had acquired 1,500 hot tubs from a German company in an inventory liquidation and had immediately sold them to a fat farm in Baja at a 300-percent profit.

So, by the time Becky Shuman arrived at Gary's Oasis for their lunch date, Gary Glass looked like a fraternity boy who had just won the beer-drinking playoffs. His light-brown hair was mussed. His cute baby face was moist. His shirt was rumpling up out of his pants; he had a twinkle in his eyes, and, Becky could also divine, a certain burning in his gut.

"Where shall we go for lunch?" Becky asked huskily. "Someplace special. After all, tonight is your big night. You're gonna be a television star."

She licked her lip gloss and crossed her legs. In their black stockings, they looked like licorice ropes, begging to be unwound. "You must be very excited," she whispered to Gary.

She was right. Between the TV commercial and the German hot-tub deal, Gary was so excited that he unwound Becky's legs and made it with her on the plush office sofa, without even taking her to lunch first. In addition, he broke two of her long, scarlet fingernails. (He did not, however, manage to mess up her hair, which was so hardened by mousse and spray that it could withstand virtually any little surprise that might happen to come up in the course of the business day.)

Meanwhile, Gary's secretary wandered through Cartier's, wondering what you buy Roberta Glass for her birthday when Roberta Glass already has everything.

■   □   ■

Roberta herself was sitting in her high-tech white-tile kitchen asking her computer what she should serve at her birthday party.

"It's my party," she said to it. "And everybody's coming to wish me a happy birthday. But really, see, it's Gary's party; it's for all our friends to see his new ad on television. He's got a new ad for Gary's Oasis. It will be aired at 10:58, 11:16, and then again at 11:52 in the middle of the 'Sick Flick' movie feature, and he wants everybody to see it. However, it would not be nice to have a party just for that, so we are using my birthday as a cover, you know what I mean? So what should we serve?"

The computer hummed.

"Party for Roberta's birthday," Roberta entered. "Request menu."

"Chocolate birthday cake," said the computer, "blintzes (subtype cheese, apple, or blueberry), Szechuan spareribs, fried rice, and gin straight up, possibly with lime."

"I told you, this only *appears* to be a party for me. It's really a party for Gary," Roberta said, "and Gary cannot eat any of those things."

"Party for Gary's television debut," she entered. "Request menu."

"One million tiny hors d'oeuvres, including little knishes, franks in blankets, shrimp with dip, avocado slices on mini tacos, sushi, decaffeinated coffee, apple juice, Coke, Perrier, and a Cuban cigar."

Roberta sighed.

"Don't forget multicolored striped marzipan cookies for your sister-in-law, Leslie," said the computer.

"Leslie swears she is not going to eat those anymore," Roberta said.

"And you *believe* that?" cried the computer in bright green letters.

Leslie arrived.

"I heard you in the street," she snapped. "You are talking to the computer again. You must get a job or you will go crazy. Come with me."

"I can't," Roberta protested. "I have to cook for Gary's party. I mean *my* party. . . ."

"Tell the computer to call the gourmet deli and

order all that stuff that Gary likes, the avocado, the shrimp, the apple juice, the usual. *You* come with me."

"Where are we going?"

Leslie pushed her out the door. "I have finally figured out what to get you for your birthday."

Roberta got excited for the first time since the preparations for her birthday had begun. But then the big surprise, the absolutely perfect present, the only thing in the world that Roberta Glass didn't have, turned out to be a total makeover at Adrian's Body Boutique, the most expensive beauty parlor in North Jersey.

For some reason, this felt to Roberta like a bit of a put-down, threatening to depress her. Therefore she tried to pay as little attention as possible while they bathed the upper half of her body in mud (*Yucch!*) and waxed her inner thighs (*Aghhhh!*) and shaved the calluses on the soles of her feet. ("Will I have anything left to walk on when this is over, Leslie?" inquired the slightly bleeding Roberta.)

The sisters-in-law experimented with red polish, pink polish, white polish, and imitation-sequoia polish, and tested maybe twenty different lipsticks on the skin of their knuckles. They heard stories of more cheating, stealing, sadomasochism, sodomy, bigamy, and litigation than Roberta would ever have dreamed possible for a small community of commuters. Helen Garfinkle was hiding from her husband, who had come back to collect his alimony payments. ("Those goddamn feminists, may they rot with their goddamn equality laws," she muttered under the drier. "If my husband calls me, Adrian, I'm not here.") Martha

Teasdale was getting ready for a very big evening: Her daughter Blanche was coming home with a lover, and of course it had turned out that the lover was another girl! How was she supposed to tell Lenny *that*? When Lenny heard that, he would fall face down in his bouillabaisse and drown!

Roberta tried to seal her ears. She read The Personals and dreamed.

On the other hand, Leslie Glass agonized over what Roberta's final "look" should be. She leafed through French beauty magazines frantically, as though she were searching for just the right mug shot of just the right rapist, consulting seriously with the manicurist, pouring out her fears and doubts to the impassive Adrian.

"Of course I would love her to change the color, Adrian," Leslie said. "But I'm scared. Look at these pictures [leaf, leaf, flip, flip]. How am I supposed to be able to tell if this color is going to go good with her eyes and her chin and her personality? Roberta is not neurotic enough for a serious change of hue."

Roberta did not even look up.

"She's not paying any attention," Adrian said. (He wasn't either.)

"Stop reading The Personals, Roberta," Leslie snapped. "You are drifting away again. Read the want ads. The *want* ads!"

Beautiful stranger, Roberta read, *red hair, green jumpsuit, walking dogs in Washington Square Park. Can't forget you. Give love a chance. Blackie.* She sighed. "Oh, I hope she gives him a chance."

"Roberta, please!" Leslie said. "He must be some kind of a pervert! What do you think of this?"

She showed Roberta a picture of a tall, thin Frenchwoman with short, reddish hair shaped like an apostrophe. She was wearing a silk tie.

"He could be sincere," Roberta insisted.

"No one named Blackie is sincere."

"But he can't forget her!" Roberta cried. "He's in love! I think it's great!"

"I thought you were reading the want ads."

"I know . . . I was," said Roberta. "I just can't seem to find . . ."

"Don't settle for anything less than fifty thousand," Leslie said, leafing and flipping.

As it happened, Leslie Glass seriously believed that her sister-in-law, Roberta, the happy housewife, could go out tomorrow and make fifty thousand a year, because Leslie had done precisely that, and with relatively little trouble. After the breakup of her marriage to "that shit," Leslie had realized that she would probably have to go to work. However, the only thing she knew how to do was shop. So, seeing that Fort Lee was a high-rise city minutes from New York, filled with high-priced professional media women who needed lots of clothes but who had absolutely no time to go shopping, Leslie founded Your Friend Leslie's Customized Buying Service.

She made friends with the anchorwomen and the soap-opera actresses, took their measurements, ascertained their goals, judged their moods, and then went shopping for their suits, hats, shoes, stockings, pocketbooks, lingerie, everything.

"Explain to me again why what you do is considered working, Les," said her brother, Gary, nastily one night while they were sitting around having grapefruit sections and playing Trivial Pursuit.

"You are such a pig, Gary," Leslie hissed. "It is not nothing to find twenty-six different outfits—not white, not black, not green, no patterns, checks, or stripes—for a size-four light-skinned black woman to wear while anchoring the six-o'clock news on a major network! I defy you to do it! I defy any of your dumb tub salesmen to do it! I am so insulted by your attitude that I am now leaving this house!" And she stalked out, whispering, "God, I don't know how you live with that jerk, Roberta."

Leslie Glass did not enjoy her success. The more money she made, the less helpless she felt; the less helpless, the more independent; the more independent, the more single; the more single, the more hysterical. Clerks in major department stores genuflected when Leslie entered. At the designer showrooms, they kept Tab and fresh lemons on ice just in case she should drop by. But did she get off on these courtesies? Was her attractive head turned in the least? Not for a minute. Because not for a minute did she forget that she was twenty-seven and, give or take a night or two here and there, now and then, essentially sleeping alone.

Leslie between men was like a designer between movies—sure, absolutely sure, she would never work again, ever. "All of my problems come from being fat," she said miserably to Roberta.

"You are not fat, Les," Roberta said, but she was really thinking about Harry and Shirl.

"I am fat!" cried Leslie. "If I don't look fat, it's because every day I rack my poor body on the crucible of deprivation! But basically I am meant to be naturally, delightfully, happily chubby. It's a genetic tendency among the women in our family. In nineteenth-century Belorussia, it was *good* to be fat, and that made the Glass girls the teen queens of Minsk! But for Leslie Glass, wanting nothing more than one more crack at marriage in Fort Lee, New Jersey, in 1985, it is an endocrine nightmare!"

Another French hairstyle caught her eye. "Oh look, Adrian, what do you think of this?" He had no reaction. "Roberta! This look is you!" Roberta also had no reaction.

"I just really wanted a trim," she said.

"No, this is your birthday present," Leslie was saying. "I want to give you something *different;* Adrian, give her something *different.*"

"Outwardly shy but inwardly seething seventh-grade teacher . . ." Roberta was reading.

"Nothing weird," Leslie was saying.

". . . seeks hunk to bring her out," Roberta was reading.

"Don't worry," Adrian was saying. "Her husband will love it."

It's true, Roberta was thinking, I *am* invisible. Here is this man Adrian making me over, and he's discussing me with my sister-in-law as though I were not even here. She sighed and allowed herself to be led to the driers. Then suddenly she saw it.

"Wow!" she cried.

"What?" said Leslie, who thought it was another hairstyle.

"Here it is, a message from Jim! *Desperately seeking Susan. Keep the faith. Tuesday, 10:00 A.M. Battery Park. Gangway One. Love, Jim.*"

"Who's Jim?" Leslie asked.

"Oh God, Tuesday—that's tomorrow!"

"Who's Susan? You *know* these people?" Leslie

pulled her head out from under the drier and peered at the newspaper.

"Jim follows Susan all over the country," Roberta explained. "Last January she was in Mexico City, then Seattle. They send messages back and forth through the personal columns in the paper. That's how they hook up. Now they're in New York."

She sagged back under the drier, smiling to herself. What must it be like to be a woman like Susan, so desired, so hunted? Oh, Roberta Glass wished that once, just once . . .

"Desperate," she said. "God, I love that word. It's so romantic."

"Everybody I know is desperate *except* you," Leslie commented.

"I'm desperate," Roberta protested.

Leslie laughed and laughed and leafed and flipped and dried and laughed. Would you listen to that Roberta! One hundred and ten pounds tops, no matter what she ate! The most successful husband under thirty-five in the greater metropolitan area! Three beautiful bathrooms! A personal pool, a personable computer, and a great maid! And she said *she* was desperate! *Ha!*

Roberta screwed up her mouth and knitted her brows, circled Jim's ad with lipstick, and made a little wish that once, just once, Leslie's hair would come out vermilion.

Immediately, she crossed her fingers and took it back and said she didn't mean it, really, truly . . . but she was enormously relieved at the end of the day when Leslie's hair came out its usual bright, light brown.

After all, you can never tell when something you

wished for casually under the drier might just come true.

■   □   ■

At about the same time that Roberta Glass was successfully retracting the curse on her sister-in-law's hair, Susan woke up in a hotel room in Atlantic City and decided to take some pictures.

No, first she would order room service.

Then she would get dressed.

Then she would take some pictures with the Polaroid that belonged to the cute guy who had his forearm flung across her belly, and who was sleeping so soundly that he probably wouldn't wake up for a couple of hours.

And then the room service would come and she would eat croissants and strawberries with peanut butter, yum, yummm, not to speak of a big bowl of Captain Crunch.

And *then* . . . well, then she would decide what to do next.

The man in bed with Susan was Bruce Meeker. She recalled that she had met him in the jangling casino, that he had bet a lot and won a lot shooting craps, that he had followed her from the slots to the disco, where he sat at the bar and watched her ass dance by with appreciation, and then brought her back to this terrific big room with red-and-white-striped brocade wallpaper and a bed that looked like you could sit on it and rule the British Empire.

They got up to stroll on the boardwalk. He took

her picture, he bought her saltwater taffy, and they went back to bed. They got up and went dancing. He showed her the pictures in his wallet (his mother, his old girlfriends, his ex–business partner in wholesale gems) and bought her a bright-red radio with earphones. Then they went back to bed.

What Susan couldn't quite remember was why she had decided to come to Atlantic City in the first place.

She flipped her strong, shapely body out of the bed and threw on her earphones and bopped into the bathroom. She hardly looked in the mirror, because she didn't have to; she knew everything she had was terrific. She had round, white, plump arms and round, white, plump thighs and a heart-shaped face and a thrilling gap between her teeth. Since she had taken a lot of belly-dancing courses in high school, she had a supple midriff that she liked to show off— every shirt she owned was cut short, and every pair of pants began below her navel.

At twenty-four, Susan had left a trail of men all across America who would swear to their grandsons that she was the single most exciting woman they had ever been with—whatever her name was, however they had met. They would never forget how tightly she had held them with her mighty dancer's legs— and how fast she had disappeared.

Susan couldn't remember any of them. Except Jimmy. Jimmy, who had not sent her a message in The Personals for a very long time. Where the hell was he? The creep! She washed her multicolored blonde-and-orange hair in the posh shower and sunned herself in the pink glow of the radiant overhead light and tried to trace her steps backward; westward.

She had been with Jimmy and his group, Dry Bones, in Seattle, where they were doing a gig at a mid-size stadium with plastic grass. Jimmy played bass guitar, sometimes drums, and arranged the music and sang bass, and every night they had full houses. It was a little boring for Susan. But then Jimmy would make such wonderful love to her that her eyes teared and she almost—almost, but not quite —told him her last name.

Then Jimmy got a terrible cold because it rained so much in Seattle. And he was lying helpless, sneezing and wheezing and blowing in the motel-room bed. And Susan knew he needed her. It was in his voice. It was in his eyes. It was in his thin, sweet face and his warm embrace. So Susan took his drum out of its case and piled her stuff into it and split.

She dripped some juice from Bruce Meeker's contact-lens bottles into her eyes and blinked. So what happened then? she wondered. Where did I go? What did I do? She opened her eyes. They were bright and clear, dark blue, tiger eyes. Right. She got out on the highway and hitched.

She was wearing her purple lace pedal pushers and her black lace bra under her white net shirt and the shiny black pyramid jacket Jimmy had won for her in Mexico. Susan loved that jacket. She wore it all the time. It was silky and glittery; the lapels were black and gold; and on the back it had a big green-and-gold pyramid with an eye on top, just like the pyramid on the dollar bill. She wore her bright-yellow high-heel boots with black-rubber car parts around the ankles. Of course, all kinds of weirdos stopped to offer her a lift, but she turned them down, waiting for Mr. Right.

Along came a convoy of cowboys heading north to the Calgary Stampede. One of them was driving a van with his horse in back. He promised that if Susan rode with him, the horse would rest his long, soft, pleasant face on her shoulder and she would be allowed to feed him carrots and cubes of sugar.

Well, this prospect was just too groovy to resist. So Susan accepted the ride, and the cowboy fell in love with her, and the horse fell in love with her, and they won a lot of blue ribbons and plenty of money at the rodeo. The cowboy gave Susan $500 of his winnings and said, "Go on now, baby, get yourself some *real* clothes."

Susan bought a black lace blouse and some white lace stockings with a white lace garter belt attached, but she couldn't find anything else that struck her as *real* in all of western Canada. So she bought a plane ticket for Chicago, where she cut six inches off the bottom of the black lace blouse and got a job as a cocktail waitress.

Okay, so now that gets me to Chicago, she said to her eyes (which she was encircling with very soft, smudgy black liner, the better to look like the queens of Egypt, whom she had always admired). So how did I get from Chicago to Atlantic City?

It came to her.

One day on the shores of Lake Michigan, a miracle had happened. A monk selling ornate crucifixes suddenly discovered there was no God. In a mad passion, he tore off his robes and his hair shirt, threw his collection of crucifixes into the lake, and ran naked into a nearby forest.

Well, Susan was no dummy.

She knew a miracle when she saw one.

She peeled to her blue lace underwear. Abandoning her bag of Cheez Doodles, she plunged fearlessly into the icy waters, rescuing crosses Greek and Ukrainian, crosses with Jesus hanging on them and crosses with Jesus hauling them, crosses with shamrocks wound around them and crosses with garlic still strung to them. When she surfaced, she had six big ones dripping around her neck. (Also she was wearing the torn sail of a boat that had once capsized in a storm on this very lake, taking the life of one brother and leaving the surviving brother to become the star of a major motion picture.)

The crowd on the lakeshore cheered. They offered Susan their coats and blankets. One of them was a nice little redheaded girl. She had saved Susan's Cheez Doodles from many would-be thieves. She said she was the math whiz of the freshman class at New Trier High School. She asked if Susan would come home with her and teach her and her girlfriends how to dress.

Well, Susan knew a windfall when it fell.

So she went home with the math whiz, who lived in a palatial lakeside mansion. "Do you really care that much about religion?" said the little girl as Susan relaxed in her living room eating Twinkies.

"No," said Susan. "But I love junk."

Susan stayed with the little redheaded math whiz and her mother for a week, during which time all the girls in the freshman class at New Trier learned to dress like Susan. One of them gave Susan a gigantic black Jewish star on a bicycle chain. Another one gave

Susan a black merry-widow bra from the fifties bought for $2 at a Winnetka garage sale. Then all the mothers of all the girls in the freshman class at New Trier took up a collection and offered Susan a ticket to anyplace she wanted to go. (She could have said she wanted to go to Thailand to watch a chess tournament and they would have paid; that's how much they wanted to see the last of Susan.) But she let them off easy. She said Newark.

Which was how she wound up in the casino at Atlantic City, pumping quarters into slots, hoping she would hit the jackpot so she wouldn't have to sleep in somebody's car.

Well, she did hit the jackpot.

Plum, plum, plum: The quarters came rushing out like the waters of Aswan. Susan was very happy and gave some of her winnings to the broke old lady with a walker at the machine on her left.

"God bless you, my child," said the old lady.

"Why not?" said Susan. The quarters were still cascading. She reached for another paper cup.

A cute guy on the other side of the bank of slot machines grabbed her hand. "I also hit the jackpot, beautiful," he said. "Let me take you dancing."

It was Bruce Meeker.

They had been together for a couple of days now, and if he didn't wake up soon, Susan figured she would split.

Finally fully dressed, she began taking pictures. She lay down on her back on the floor and took a picture of herself with her most sexy look, scarlet lips parted, eyes half shut. It came out pretty good. She put it in the pocket of her pyramid jacket and crawled quietly toward Bruce.

She tickled the bottoms of his feet. Bruce shifted in his sheets so that Susan could have gotten a great shot of his powerful thighs and his adorable butt end, but she figured she wouldn't know whose butt end it was in a couple of weeks anyway, so she took a picture of his face, so sweet and innocent in sleep, and left it on his pillow as a wake-up present.

Room service knocked with breakfast and the New York *Mirror*. Susan opened the door and took a picture of the bell hop. He was young and white. He looked as though he could sing backup for the Mormon Tabernacle Choir. Susan grinned wickedly at him while the picture oozed out of the camera, developed but still wet. She tucked it in his pocket. Then she gave him $20 from Bruce's fat wallet. "Don't spend it all in one place," she said breathily.

The bell hop staggered out, leaning on the room-service cart for support.

Susan relaxed and read The Personals.

"Jimmy . . ." she whispered, for there it was, just what she had been waiting for. *Desperately seeking Susan*, it said. *Keep the faith. Tuesday, 10:00 A.M. Battery Park. Gangway One. Love, Jim.* She laughed. Her heart actually flipped. She got all damp underneath her clothes. It's about time, she said to herself, drawing a valentine around the personal with her black eyeliner.

So into the Dry Bones drum case went her assorted frocks and accessories, some crap table chips, a couple of postcards, an ashtray, her box of saltwater taffy, the silverware from the room-service tray, two towels, and a blanket. She piled her hair up under the black hat with the brass chain Jimmy had bought her at the bullfights and went through the pockets of Bruce's pants, which were thrown over the chair. He had a picture of her leaning against the railing by the beach. Really it was a picture of her ass. She laughed and left it behind for Bruce to remember her by. He had a wad of money in his wallet—Susan took only one casino-crisp $100 bill. Then, really by accident, her fingers stumbled over a handkerchief all neatly folded. Tucked inside was a pair of absolutely terrific earrings, very big. "Nice," Susan murmured, and she packed them, too.

By now the drum case was so full that it took all her strength to close it. She memorized Jim's Personal and left the newspaper by her croissants. She left Bruce's Polaroid on the bed next to him, shoved her new radio and earphones into a yellow plastic tote bag, and headed out.

"Bye, bye, Bruce," she whispered at the door of Room 1313. "It was fun, huh?"

As soon as Susan got out into the hall, the drum case opened and everything fell on the floor.

The elevator arrived.

"Shit!" cried Susan, frantically repacking. "Hold the elevator!"

A blond man came out of the elevator. He did not stop to help her, for he was not by nature a gallant man. He just walked on by, his head lowered. He wore orthopedic black-leather-and-gray-suede shoes. They squeaked, like doors. Peering sneakily under his own ear, he waited for Susan to get it all back together and rush onto the elevator. Then he continued on to Room 1313, where he suspected he might find his old friend Bruce Meeker.

The blond man never saw Susan's face. But he got a good look at the pyramid on the back of her jacket.

■   □   ■

All the Yuppies in Fort Lee came to Roberta's party that night. To Roberta, most of them were strangers. But they told her she looked beautiful in her pale-pink dress and the new pearl-and-pink-crystal necklace from Cartier that Gary had given her and the new hairstyle from Adrian's that Leslie had given her. She passed among her guests as in a dream, munching on a celery stick, holding a tray of tiny hors d'oeuvres which the strangers picked at without stopping their conversation, as though the tray carrier were invisible.

Leslie grabbed a multicolored striped marzipan cookie. "Don't let me eat these," she commanded, eating it. "They're *so good!* I think I've found one."

"One what?" Roberta asked.

"Upstairs. Come on."

Leslie grabbed Roberta's hand and pulled her up the stairs through the crowd. "Over there," she said. "He's been giving me the eye all night. Who is he?"

"Who?" said Roberta. She just couldn't quite grasp anything Leslie was saying.

"In the corner, near Gary," Leslie hissed.

Gary was in the corner chatting up a tall, dark, smart woman with blood-red fingernails. The woman's small chest was as exposed as it could possibly be on a Monday evening in Fort Lee. Roberta wondered who she was trying to hook—maybe Roberta knew, but did she really care?

"I don't know that woman," Roberta said.

"Not her!" Leslie fumed. "The guy, with the long, curly hair . . . laid back, leaning against the wall."

"Oh, that's Larry Stillman," Roberta said. "Doctor Stillman."

Leslie gasped and clutched Roberta's arm. "Plastic surgery?"

"He's Gary's dentist."

"Well, at least he's not a PhD." Off went Leslie, hot as a laser beam.

"Who's your friend, Gary?" she asked her brother. Gary Glass had never been too brilliant at noticing the sexual objectives of any woman, least of all his own sister, so he thought she meant Becky Shuman, and he started to introduce them.

But Leslie didn't look at Becky. She just inhaled Doctor Stillman like a long drink of water, and by the time Gary caught on, the laid-back dentist and the hysterical shopper were drifting off together toward what was to be a very warm relationship.

Gary's watch alarm went off. "Time out, everybody!" he yelled. "I've got a ten–fifty-eight spot."

Instantly the whole party stopped jabbering and mingling and nibbling and arranged itself before the television.

A newscaster appeared on the screen saying ". . . and the search continues for suspects in the recent robbery of ancient Egyptian artifacts. . . ." Roberta didn't pay any attention. She wandered over to the terrace, slid the glass doors aside, and stepped out into the cool night air. The great bridge lay before her like a tiara.

Gary's commercial came on, but she didn't turn to watch. There he was on the stony shores of a hot tub, in a safari suit and a pith helmet, saying, "Hi, I'm

Gary from Gary's Oasis! In our New Jersey show-room we have hundreds of models. . . ." Bikini-clad actresses from Becky's casting agency splashed around him, giggling mischievously. "We're open seven days a week . . ." Gary was saying. The breeze from the Hudson made Roberta's earrings swing and stirred her neglected heart. "Hey, Gary, come on in!" the pretty bathers yelled. Then they pulled him, fully clothed, into the bubbling waters as he cried, "Come to Gary's Oasis! Where all your fantasies come true!"

The party guests cheered and applauded and kissed Becky Shuman and congratulated Gary Glass.

Roberta paid no attention. As far as she was concerned, her house was filled with strangers. To them she was invisible. Okay. So be it. She let her imagination loose like a magic bird on the night air, and it carried her far, far away into a real-life fantasy.

■   □   ■

She imagined that Susan was at that very moment on her way to meet Jim, crossing the glittering George Washington Bridge to New York City, stepping off a bus at the Port Authority. And she was right, that's exactly what Susan was doing.

Despite the fact that the Port Authority Bus Terminal looked like a plastic milk crate, it was in Susan's experience one of the most terrific places to get dressed in all Manhattan. It had long, plastic seats where you could doze off when you had no place to sleep, and if the cops bothered you, you could tell them you were a commuter who had missed her bus, and as long as you weren't armed or high or drunk or mentally deranged, they would be happy to believe you.

The ladies' room was sensational. It had a wide shelf under a long mirror where Susan could spread out all her stuff without bugging anybody else. At midnight, there were at least six other women fixing themselves at the long shelf, getting ready for Tuesday morning in the Big Apple. Every one of them was complaining about men.

Susan washed her armpits and gave herself a little rush by drying them with the warm-air blower that doesn't chap your skin like an icky old paper towel. Then she dumped some of her stuff on the wide shelf. She changed from her black net shirt into her pink net shirt, from her black lace bra to her other black net. She repinned her hair, added some black eyeliner around her eyes, and, just for fun, blackened the little mole above her mouth so it looked like a beauty mark. She made sure her lipstick was luscious enough.

Finally, she added just one of the big earrings she had swiped from Bruce Meeker's handkerchief.

In her drum case Susan had a postcard from a place called the Magic Club, way downtown. Once, awhile back, she had worked there, and if her luck held her old friend Crystal might still be assisting the main magician. Susan was hoping that Crystal would be willing to put her up for tonight at least, and maybe also for the foreseeable future.

She tried to recall whether she had done anything really terrible the last time she had stayed with Crystal.

Had she stolen the front door?

No, that was in Biloxi.

Had she put eyeliner on the cat?

No, that was in Bangor.

Had she thrown one of her famous parties?

No, that was on a big farm near Nashville owned by the grandparents of a sweet kid who had the crazy notion that someday she would become the queen of evangelical rock.

Whatever Susan had done the last time she stayed with Crystal, she just couldn't recall how bad it was. So she decided to stash her drum case in a locker and head south to the Magic Club.

For the first time during this leg of her journey, Susan now had a little problem.

The locker cost a quarter, and all she had were two subway tokens and the $100 bill.

She rummaged through the inner pockets of her pyramid jacket. She found a nail file. She jimmied the lock on the locker, stuffed her stuff inside, and pocketed the key. It was a standard silver key with a red plastic cap, instantly recognizable to people who know how terrific the New York Port Authority terminal really is.

■   □   ■

In Fort Lee, Roberta Glass hung out in her kitchen, wearing white silk pajamas, sleepless, disconsolate.

Her many guests had left long ago. She watched Laurence Olivier and Joan Fontaine having their great love affair in *Rebecca* on the television. She picked at what remained of her birthday cake, a

whipped-cream cake with cherry filling, not her favorite (but it was nice of Leslie to remind Gary to
order it). She wondered what Susan was doing at this
moment. Probably meeting her lover. Probably dancing the night away. Something exciting. Something
romantic.

Gary came in to take his vitamins.

"If you want to watch TV, you can watch in the
bedroom with the earphones," he said.

"I don't want to watch TV," she said, watching
TV.

"People really liked my commercial, don't you
think?"

"Yes, they did, they loved it. You were terrific."

He smiled to himself. Roberta thought that he had
a smile just like his late father's smile, very confident.
She had always felt safe and cared for with Gary, like
a little girl.

"Do you ever remember your dreams?" she asked.

"Dreams? Oh, sure. They're all coming true. Now,
don't forget, tomorrow you've got to pick up the new
radio for the car," he told her. "Tell the guy you're
my wife, because we're gonna put a sauna in his
apartment and he's gonna give us a really great
price."

"It's gone forever," said Laurence Olivier, cradling
Joan Fontaine's face in his hands. "That funny,
young, lost look I loved. It won't ever come back."

Is it gone forever? Roberta thought, watching Gary
gobble his pills. The safe, the cared for, the little girl?
Won't it ever come back?

"Night, hon," he said, patting her on the head.
"Don't eat all that cake."

■　□　■

The same old derelict had been lying on the pavement outside the Magic Club for as long as anybody could remember.

He never snored. He never shifted. Patrons sometimes tripped over him on their way home. He never awoke, even if they apologized. He was like a lot of the garbage that collected in the very dark, silent streets outside the Magic Club: fixed. If it rained, he got wet. If it snowed, he got covered up. But he stayed where he was. Henry, the octogenarian pianist who led the band at the Magic Club, said to Max the septuagenarian saxophonist on the occasion of the ninetieth birthday of Vito the drummer that maybe the derelict was dead.

But if he was dead, why didn't he smell?

Like the fixed derelict and the garbage on the pavement, like Henry and Max and Vito, nothing at the Magic Club ever changed much. Costumes from previous habitations still hung on the racks in the ladies' dressing room. The capes of magicians who had made themselves disappear long ago were draped over the shoulders of life-size cardboard figures of Claudette Colbert and Wonder Woman. They had resided in the dressing room since rent control.

"I myself have had many bizarre sexual encounters with these classic beauties," said Kaminsky the dummy. Kaminsky was the star of the curtain-raising act of the Magic Show program. He lived in a suitcase. He was a real dummy. He had thinning red hair and plaid pants. His legs flopped. Kaminsky complained constantly about his ventriloquist, who was always shutting him up before his stories got too dirty. For example, as soon as Kaminsky began to elaborate on his erotic experiences with Wonder Woman and Claudette Colbert, the suitcase snapped shut on his upper lip.

Henry, Max, and Vito remembered strippers with sequined nipples who had played the Magic Club before it was the Magic Club, blues singers with feathers on their heads, actors who were now Hollywood regulars who broke their teeth on Strindberg and Ibsen on the Magic Club's exhausted little stage. They remembered with particular delight a band of transvestite ballet dancers who wore big blonde wigs and peach-gray tutus. Although the performers had vanished, the sequins and the feathers and the (small-breasted) tutus hung on. Two tutus in particular were still being worn, along with a big blonde wig, by Susan's old friend Crystal.

Crystal had met Susan during a Duran Duran concert in Cleveland. Crystal wanted a T-shirt, but they were too expensive. She tried to swipe one, but she had never been too fast on her feet. So of course the security men grabbed her. Crystal started to cry. Susan popped out from behind a hot-dog stand, snatched the T-shirt, and disappeared into the crowd. So of course the security men threatened to arrest Crystal.

She cried so much that they settled for throwing her out of the concert. Crystal didn't know what to do. She couldn't go home, because Maine was too far away. She couldn't go back to the convent where she was staying, because she had promised Sister Dolores a Duran Duran T-shirt and could not bear to disappoint nice people. She was perfectly miserable, sitting on a curb, watching her tears run with the rainwater down into the sewers.

Miraculously, Susan popped out from behind a mailbox. "I've got something for you," she said. She handed Crystal not one but *four* T-shirts and an autographed program. That was all it took. Crystal became her friend for life.

The two girls hitched to New York together. In six months, they had twenty-seven jobs between them. Crystal's big breakthrough came when Ian the magician, Master of Illusion, headliner at the Magic Club for as long as anybody could remember, hired her as his assistant. She got Susan a job helping to tend bar. But Ian the magician didn't like Susan. He thought she was a bad influence on Crystal. So he was happy when Susan went off with Jimmy to Seattle.

Crystal really missed Susan.

Somehow everyone seemed to fall asleep when Susan left town.

"The customers at the Magic Club are as sleepy as the derelict lying out front," she wrote to Susan on the postcard that Susan kept in her drum case. "They never laugh. They never clap. If they look at me at all, it's only when my boobies falls out of that damn strapless (small-breasted) tutu. The other night I tripped off the stage and landed on my ass, and they all sat around waiting for somebody else to pick me up. For God's sake, *come home!* Your friend, Crystal."

There were two waitresses at the Magic Club. They sold drinks and cigarettes. One of them leaned against the wall for hours on end and looked like a Eurasian mannequin. Many customers did not believe she was real. They hung their hats on her and stamped out their cigarettes on the toes of her red shoes.

The other waitress moved, but very slowly, passing among the tables like a restless wraith through a graveyard. "Filters," she murmured. "Non-filters, extrathins, extralongs, superlights, high-test, premium, unleaded . . ."

Ray, the Magic Club's manager and emcee, wore a bronze tuxedo jacket he had rented for his prom in 1962 and never returned. He told jokes so old they predated the president's film career. He referred to his audience as "ladies and germs." His mother, Gilda, the head bartender, was wont to say that the Magic Club contained more antiques than the Frick Museum and should be declared a historical monument. She wrote as much to the mayor. But for some reason, her letter was forwarded to the Welfare Department and a social worker came to visit.

The miracle was that the Magic Club survived. Ray made a living, and so did Ian and Crystal and the band and the waitresses, and Kaminsky the dummy made enough to pay his ventriloquist's child support.

"This is because we provide an essential service," Gilda the motherly bartender explained. "Pressured New Yorkers always need a quiet place with deep shadows where they can just stare into space and take a little rest and think nothing."

Onstage, Ian the magician was tossing gold rings to Crystal in the final throes of their act. Drum roll: She dropped the first ring. Drum roll: The second one rolled by her. Drum roll: The third ring she actually caught. The musicians were so astounded, they played a chord. The curtain fell.

Crystal stumbled and groped her way backstage to

the ladies' dressing room, bumped into Wonder Woman, stepped on Claudette Colbert, and felt her way along the rubbish-strewn dressing table until at last, at last, she found her glasses.

Oh, happiness! The light dawned! The once-dim world of shadowy fuzz burst upon Crystal in brilliant Technicolor! In Panavision! In black parachute-silk pants and still smoking!

"Susan! My God, Susan, we thought you were dead!"

"No, just in New Jersey."

Crystal and Susan hugged and kissed.

"Anybody I know?" Crystal asked.

"Oh, some guy from Atlantic City," Susan said. "It was fun until he started getting serious."

Crystal laughed and threw her wig on a Styrofoam head, wriggled out of her tutu and into a different dress (originally worn by Belinda What's-Her-Face in the animal act she did before she got into serious porn, Mother Gilda said). "I am ready to quit this dump," Crystal bitched, wriggling. "Ray won't let me wear my glasses onstage, and then Ian gets pissed off because I can't do any of the tricks. I mean I am *only* legally blind! I could understand if I wanted to wear my glasses on my tits, but nobody in this dive is looking at my face anyway. . . . Could you zip me up?"

"Oh come on, Crystal," Susan said, "let's just get out of here."

"But I've still got to do the Mystery of the Disappearing Blue Bird! Can't you wait a few minutes?"

"Look, I'm really tired," Susan said. "Why don't I get some pizza and I'll meet you at home."

Crystal brightened. "You got a place?"

"Not exactly," Susan said, chewing her lip. "But I'm working on it. . . ." She grinned.

"Oh, no . . ." Crystal said.

"Just for tonight. Come on, I promise. Come on. . . ."

Crystal scowled and repinned her thick, wavy, nicely graying hair. "Do you promise, only seven-digit phone calls?"

Oh, *that* was what I did last time I was at Crystal's, Susan remembered. "Cross my heart," she said. She gave Crystal another big hug and kiss, and Crystal (knowing full well that she would probably regret it) gave her the key to her apartment.

Crystal got home at 3:30 A.M. to find that Susan had redecorated.

She had painted a couple of walls canary yellow to match Crystal's favorite tights. She had swiped a potted tree from the West Twenties. It stood now on Crystal's coffee table, which Susan had covered with a Russian shawl that had wonderful, graceful fringes.

"I love the shawl!" squealed Crystal. "Where'd you get it?"

"It slipped off a woman who was kissing her boyfriend on Duane and Reade."

"Oh, Susan . . ."

"Eat your pizza."

"Where'd you get the pizza?"

"It fell off a . . ."

"Don't tell me!" Crystal screamed. "Tell me about the guy in Atlantic City. . . . Tell me about Dry Bones; I heard they're cutting a real record. Tell me about the palatial lakeside mansion in Chicago. . . ."

Susan told her everything. Crystal told Susan

everything. They gossiped and giggled until dawn and fell asleep in their clothes.

The next morning Susan got all dressed up and followed her heart to Battery Park and Jimmy.

She bopped into a guy who was buying a newspaper from a machine. He took a long look at her. She smiled. "Oh well, baby," he crooned, "why don't you just take a paper?" Susan kept smiling. She took all the papers and dropped them disdainfully at his feet. He backed off fast. "I mean, some of these broads you meet in the streets of New York are really terrifying," he said to his buddies that night in the pool hall.

Susan had not intended to read the paper, since she only read the paper if there was going to be a personal from Jimmy, and on this beautiful morning Jimmy was waiting for her at the Battery. But the front page knocked her out. It had a large picture of Bruce Meeker, crushed and bleeding and totally dead on the boardwalk.

MOBSTER FALLS FROM HOTEL WINDOW; MYSTERY WOMAN SOUGHT FOR QUESTIONING, said the headline.

"Shit," said Susan.

■　□　■

Jimmy Riddle, the bass guitarist, sometime drummer, arranger, and bass singer for Dry Bones, sat on a bench at the Battery. He was wearing his green-and-black band jacket and looking for the woman he loved. A sensitive, thin young man, not yet thirty, Jimmy was already a little beat up from his many years on the rock circuit. His brown hair stuck up in spikes. His eyes were gentle and intelligent; they could break a girl's heart.

A long time ago, Jimmy had spent one whole year being stoned. Then his father died and he had to go home to Flagstaff for the funeral. All his brothers were there. His mother asked him to sing. But he couldn't sing because he had been stoned for a year. His mother thought grief had made him songless. But she had never understood Jimmy anyway, even though she loved him a lot. She didn't understand that it's grief that makes a man sing and that it was coke that made her Jimmy dumb.

He hadn't done any drugs since that day, because he felt he already had enough to be ashamed of.

The guys in Dry Bones, who had been Jimmy's best friends in college before they all quit school together, seemed to be falling a little out of synch with him. They said he was getting older and they were staying young. In fact, they had always been younger than Jimmy, and they were all exactly the same age.

If the band made a good living, it was because Jimmy knew how to hire a manager and fire one, too. If the band didn't get stale, it was because Jimmy listened to other people's music and never stopped learning. If the band didn't break up, it was because Jimmy stuck with Dry Bones, even though he was offered spots in bigger groups. He had a loyal streak. It was why he would have to wait to get rich. It was why Dry Bones would one day be very, very famous.

Jimmy had a secret that he had never told anybody except his best friend, Dez O'Herlihy. As a kid, he had been fat. Really fat, he told Dez; roly-poly. He couldn't sit on a horse without rolling off. He couldn't explore a cave without getting stuck. His brothers were all major jocks, but not Jim. He could huff and puff and pray, but his fat legs would not carry him safely to first base no matter how far he had hit the ball. "I never beat the throw," he told Dez, "not once, not once."

Jimmy's pitch was perfect, and his voice never changed; it was always low, from babyhood. The high-school music teacher came out to the house and told Jimmy's parents he had real talent and should attend a conservatory, maybe in the East. He could get a scholarship, he could go far. "His name was Wayne Hammerford," Jimmy told Dez. "He taught me piano. He gave me the baritone solos in *The Messiah*. I don't think he was ever out of Flagstaff."

Jimmy's mother believed everything Mr. Hammerford said about her roly-poly son and settled her certitude on Jimmy quietly, like an extra blanket on a cold desert night. But Jimmy's father was ashamed of him. And he loved his father; his father was a cowboy and a really great guy.

Because he was so fat, he sympathized with the other kids who had things wrong with them and were having a hard time in high school. He sympathized with the clumsy goons. He sympathized with the dipshits. Most of all he sympathized with the very smart kids, who always had the worst time of all.

So even after Jimmy lost fifty pounds—in his senior year of high school—and came up lean and muscular as a quarter-horse herder, the insecurities and sensitivities he had learned as a fat kid stayed with him and made him successful in the wide world.

Very smart people, who wouldn't ordinarily drink two beers with an itinerant rock musician, felt comfortable with Jimmy and agreed to represent him and his group and set them up with hot chick singers. Melancholy folk poets with great lyrics in their hearts gave Jimmy their songs. He could do a blues number real well, real well, and if it was late at night, and all the bullshit had stopped, Jimmy Riddle could get the truth out of anyone. Even Susan.

He stretched his long arms out on the back of the bench in the warm June sunshine. The citizens of Lower Manhattan strolled by, all colors and sizes, like a bunch of flowers, a beautiful sight for any artist to behold. But Jimmy didn't take much note of them. All he wanted was to see Susan again.

He worried that she might have missed his Personal, that she might not have received his message, that she might still be in Canada someplace with that horse she liked so much. He worried that, even if she had seen his ad, she might be too far away to make it to the Battery on time. And Jimmy didn't have much time. Dry Bones was doing a concert in Buffalo this very evening, and the van would be by to pick him up in less than an hour, and he wanted to ask Susan to come with him to Buffalo. He kind of knew she would say no. But he had to give it a try. In the worst way, he didn't want to play another college tour without her.

A really pretty woman sat down on the adjacent bench. She had shiny, bright-blonde hair and a nice overbite. She wore a little white blouse and white pants and a pink sweater, looked like an out-of-towner in the summer punk crowd. To Jimmy, she seemed nervous, fidgety; he figured she was waiting for someone. He asked her for a match. She didn't have one and didn't seem to want to talk, seemed scared, as though she thought he might be trying to pick her up.

Well, she wasn't so far off base; not too long ago, he would indeed have tried to pick her up. Lately he just didn't have the inclination. All he could think about was the crazy, funny girl he had met in a luncheonette twenty blocks north of here. She was a waitress. She busted out of her silly yellow uniform like popcorn. When he came in to eat, she took off her shades and grinned—what did she have wrapped around her head? Old blue dance tights! She looked him up. She leaned over the counter and looked him down. She wrote her phone number in eyeliner on his napkin. Then she crushed the napkin and stuffed it in his coffee.

What a napkin that was! So absorbent! Such incredible tensile strength! She squeezed it out and spread it out and, believe it or not, he could still read the phone number!

When Jimmy tried to pay for his breakfast, the waitress winked and tore up his check very slowly. One by one she stuffed the little pieces in her cleavage.

She was fired on the spot.

Jimmy took her out and bought her breakfast. She ordered Captain Crunch.

When had all that happened . . . two years ago? Three years? Was it really three years that he had been chasing Susan?

"Susan!" he yelled, spying her pyramid jacket as she leaned against the railing by the water. And off he ran.

The pretty blonde woman with the pink sweater

ran after him, looking for the lucky creature who answered to that magic name. But Jimmy was too fast for her. She lost him in the crowd. So she put a quarter into one of the coin-operated binoculars placed along the promenade for viewing the Statue of Liberty and scanned the shore like Charlton Heston at his periscope, panning by kids and running dogs frolicking and a whole boatload of day cruisers from a software convention. And then suddenly she had her fantasy couple in sight. Jim and Susan.

Jim picked Susan up and sat her on the railing by the bay and kissed her with more passion than Roberta had ever been kissed with in her whole, entire life. Susan locked her legs around Jimmy and he stroked her thighs, and they didn't care who saw them.

Back at the Oasis, Gary Glass was very busy becoming the spa king of New Jersey. He had no idea that his shy, repressed wife, Roberta, was at Battery Park, watching Susan and Jim grope each other by the choppy waters of the bay.

Gary thought Roberta was spending her day getting a fancy radio installed in his car.

Gary thought Roberta was easily satisfied.

What the hell did Gary know?

Chapter 2

Jimmy Riddle did not leave Susan with a quiet heart.

Of course, she had refused to go with him to Buffalo—she said it would be boring—he had anticipated that. But then she showed him a newspaper clipping that activated all the mature things about him, including his ulcer.

"You were with this guy?!" he exclaimed, noting Bruce Meeker's smashed face, his twisted, broken limbs.

"He was breathing when I left," Susan offered lightly.

"This is serious," Jimmy said. "Mainstream serious. I don't like leaving you."

"I can take care of myself," Susan countered.

Well, that was probably true, too. Jimmy had seen Susan pour her drink over a very evil-looking motorcycle freak just because she didn't like the way he talked about her crucifixes.

A big impresario brought Dry Bones to Orlando. He was supposed to pay all expenses. After three concerts, he reneged and tried to stick the band with the hotel bill. Susan smeared, but *carefully* smeared, an entire gallon of hot taco sauce on the inside of the impresario's big silver car.

A record-company executive had put the make on Jimmy at a party. Fine-looking woman, he told his friend Dez. Thin legs. Backless dress. Small, bright eyes. Susan quietly told this executive to lay off. The woman laughed in her face. She allowed Susan to watch as she slipped her fingers into the back pocket of Jimmy's jeans and copped a feel. Susan took offense. Arming herself with a kitchen knife, she cornered the fine-looking record-company executive in the bathroom and threatened to slit open her nose.

"How did you even *think* of something like that?" Jimmy asked.

"I saw it in a movie," Susan answered.

"But would you have done it?"

"*She* thought I would have done it. That's all that counts, Mr. Irresistible."

Okay. So Susan had proved herself to be a tough customer. However, certain situations might prove even tougher than Susan, might lie beyond solution by bluff or bravado or trumped-up movie threats, and the case of Bruce Meeker might be a case in point. The newspaper said Meeker was a "mobster." Jimmy had his own recollections of what *they* were like.

Once the lead guitarist in Dry Bones had accepted a gig on a yacht off the Carolina coast. A big private party: southern gentry, good pay. The pay was so good, in fact, that Jimmy felt suspicious.

"Dry Bones doesn't need a mob party," he said.

"You know, you ought to get some therapy, Jim," answered the lead guitarist. "You worry too much."

But the sailors who came in launches to collect the band had guns in their belts.

It turned out to be a great party. The champagne popped and bubbled. The southern gentry bopped and bubbled. The host gave away coke spoons as party favors, and there was free toot in the sugar bowls along with the Sweet 'N Low. But Jimmy didn't take an easy breath until Dry Bones got back to the mainland. The next day they heard that after the party had ended, some other guys with guns in their belts had boarded the yacht. And a lot of people who had been dancing and singing and shouting requests to the band only hours before did not live to see the dawn.

Now Jimmy was supposed to calmly ride off the Battery in his band's green-and-black van painted all over with skulls and skeletons and leave Susan with the same class of person maybe following her, maybe hunting her, maybe ready to nail her just because she knew this poor stiff on the boardwalk.

"Let me give you a phone number," he said.

"Don't bother, I'm fine."

"I'm giving you this number. It belongs to a friend of mine named Dezmund O'Herlihy; call him Dez."

"I don't need your numbers," Susan said petulantly. "Next time, if you're only going to be in town for an hour, don't put an ad in The Personals."

"Take the number," he said, writing it on the back of the newspaper article. "Dez is a great guy. If you really get in a jam, give him a call. He'll know how to reach me."

Susan laughed and put Dez O'Herlihy's number in her jacket pocket.

"Has he got any money?" she asked.

"Forget it," Jimmy said. "He knows all about you."

The Dry Bones van pulled up. Jimmy jumped in and took the wheel. Susan ran alongside, holding his hand. Through the window she looked like a pretty little Christmas tree to him. She looked like a lot of candles on a cake. Everything about her shined and glittered, and it wasn't even dark.

"Be here the next time I get back," Jimmy said, as the van pulled away. In the rearview mirror he saw her waving. He had a vision of a mobster pointing a stubby black gun at all the places he liked to kiss Susan, at her soft, white neck; at her blue tiger eyes; and at her laughing, pouting mouth. He wanted to turn the van around and scoop her up off the Battery and cram her into the seat next to him and keep her there. But he was afraid to crowd her. He didn't want to make her think he was afraid to crowd her. He didn't want to make her think he was hovering over her or trying to protect her or getting serious about her or anything, because every time he did that, she split on him.

So he *didn't* call Dezmund O'Herlihy from the road.

He *didn't* say, "I'm worried about my girl, Susan. She's mixed up with the friggin' mob; she may be in trouble. Go find her, hover over her, protect her, because I'm in love with her, and that's the honest-to-God truth."

Somewhere on the New York Thruway, Jimmy gave up the wheel and napped in the van. It was hot. He crashed at a motel in another suburb. He tried to act his age and forget Susan and think exclusively about playing and singing bass.

■   □   ■

Susan herself was feeling a little disappointed about Jimmy's quick departure—they hadn't even had time to make love or dance all night or drink even one tequila sunrise. So to make it up to herself for having to endure the pangs of heartbreak so early in the morning, she decided to go shopping.

Roberta Glass decided to follow her.

Roberta personally had a terror of shopping and did it as little as possible. But she just *had* to see what Susan would buy, what she wanted, what she needed. (Kaminsky the dummy said to Claudette Colbert and Wonder Woman in the Magic Club that, in hindsight, it was clear that Roberta's shopping neurosis lay at the root of her fascination with Susan and her ultimate involvement with Bruce Meeker's murderer, but the suitcase closed before he had a chance to explain further.)

Roberta's mother had been one of the most eminent shoppers in the Boston-Baltimore megalopolis. She made it her business to teach Roberta everything, but everything, about the craft.

She showed Roberta how to rummage among string beans and detect the limp ones by touch. She taught her how to sniff for ripeness of canteloupe and the freshness of chopped liver.

"Always turn everything upside down and inside out, sweetheart baby," she told Roberta. "Never buy a coat with a cheesy lining or a dress with a skimpy hem. If you are buying a piece of furniture, be sure to examine the flip side. If it's an 800-pound sofa, ask the salesman to turn it over. Then bounce your car keys on the underfacing of the upholstery. If they don't tear through, start to bargain."

Roberta's mother loved bargains more than anything in the whole world. If she saw a special on $5 fake mother-of-pearl compacts, she would buy four and save them for occasions requiring meaningless presents. ("It's the thought that counts," she counseled.) She did the same thing with veal breast for stuffing. Neither Roberta nor her father, or, for that matter, her mother, particularly liked stuffed breast of veal. But taste be damned, if the price was right, Mom bought in bulk.

The joke whose punchline went "For $10 let it hang in the closet" was invented to describe Roberta's mother. She dressed like a Bess Myerson clone, kept enough food on hand to feed—should they happen to attack—the Egyptian Third Army, and still never overspent her housekeeping allowance.

When Roberta was a little child of six, her mother introduced her to the Osterfein Experience.

Miguel Osterfein and Aunts was a small chain of clothing stores, famous for its discounts on better women's wear. There was an Osterfein's in the lush Philadelphia suburb where Roberta grew up, another Osterfein's in the lush Boston suburb where she went to school, another just off the Baltimore-Washington Beltway in case you needed something to do while your car was parked for six hours in traffic. And there was also an Osterfein's in the New Jersey Meadowlands in the shadow of Giants Stadium, not a stone's throw from the shadow of the Byrne Arena.

Each Osterfein's had several large dressing rooms where a woman could take no more than six items to try on, having made her selection from the huge stock on the floor. The dressing rooms contained no partitions. They were lined with mirrors. They had little benches where you could put the clothes you had worn to come to Osterfein's, the mother you had brought along who would eventually pay for what you bought, the little girl you had brought along so she could watch and learn the shape of her life to come.

Ah, the shapes in Osterfein's dressing rooms! They boggled the mind of the impressionable youngster. Since in the mid-sixties, when Roberta was six, there were few health clubs, it was here that she learned all the different kinds of bodies she might develop. Watching her mother slip in and out of suits with maimed labels (the better to hide their true designer origins while at the same time suggesting that they really did have designer origins to hide), she learned that even if you were thin you could have stretch marks; even if you were fat you could be beautiful; even if you were a member of the leisure class, your legs could turn blue.

Most Osterfeins' in Roberta's experience contained at least one supervisory saleswoman named Ceil, pronounced "Seal." She wore nurse's shoes. She wore glasses on a chain around her neck. She enforced the house rule, that like the American flag, no Osterfein's item must ever touch the floor. God forbid you step out of a dress you were trying on and got it dusty—

Ceil would have you ejected in shame. Periodically she cried out in a voice like wheels skidding: "Ova the head, ladies! Ova the head!"

Although no one could ever prove it, the rumor persisted that at the end of the business day, when all the customers were gone, a brigade of secret cleaners would enter the dressing rooms and wash away all the blood that had been spilled there during battles between mothers who shrieked, "I wouldn't be caught dead in that rag!" and daughters who shrieked back, "Everything you own makes you look dead, *Motherrrr!*"

Roberta never fought with her mother. First of all, she was too shy and repressed to do that, even as a child. Second, she liked her mother and thought that her mother probably knew best. Wasn't it true that every time Mom told her to wear a coat and she didn't she was cold?

So it took extraordinary courage for Roberta to say as a tender preteen that, even though her mother wanted her to dress like Jackie Onassis, Roberta wanted to dress like Marilyn Monroe.

"Oh, my poor baby!" cried Mom, hugging Roberta and kissing her. "Don't you realize, a good shopper doesn't wear what she wants. A good shopper wears what they're showing. I understand how much you admire Marilyn Monroe, my sweet little angel baby, but when you're shopping, it's really better not to model yourself after women who kill themselves before they're forty."

This really scared the hell out of Roberta.

She went back to keeping her mouth shut and thereafter agreed to wear whatever her mother picked out for her. (Ten years later, Gary Glass would recount that he first noticed Roberta because something about her reminded him of Jackie Onassis, a woman whose husbands he idolized.)

Up until the early seventies, Osterfein's had remained a largely Hebraic secret, shrouded in cabalistic mystery. But then, suddenly, the secret got out, and the whole customer profile at Osterfein's changed radically.

In came upscale black girls who wanted to dress like Angela Davis, with mothers who wanted them to dress like Gladys Knight. New blood stained the dressing-room floors. In came mysteriously rich immigrants from Russia and Asia. They had never seen so much stock in their lives and often went into abundance shock, passing out among the jumpsuits. Ceil had to revive them with tea and Sara Lee banana cake in her private chambers. In came stately WASPs. Only yesterday they'd been flower children skinny-dipping at Woodstock. Now they were the wives of rising technocrats. They were ready to go back to shopping as long as they didn't have to look like their *motherrrrs*. Osterfein's was the logical answer.

Neither Miguel Osterfein nor any of his aunts really understood this phenomenal change. They asked marketing experts and demographic experts, but nobody had an explanation. They should have asked Kaminsky the dummy. A student of history and a great lover of women, Kaminsky realized that the panculturalization of the Osterfein Experience had occurred because in the seventies, women had begun sharing secrets with each other, especially on Wednesday nights. All these broads from all these different ethnic groups would get together, Kaminsky explained to the derelict at the Magic Club, something they called consciousness-raising meetings, very much in vogue in those days. Everybody thought they were discussing politics. Not entirely, said Kaminsky. They were also discussing Osterfein's.

As a result of the same huge information exchange, Kaminsky continued, the classic Osterfein's customer pool began to shudder and shake and fray at the edges.

One of the frays turned out to be Roberta's mother.

On a certain Thursday when Roberta was sixteen, Mom went to Osterfein's without her little sweetheart baby girl. She said she was going to buy a dress to wear to a bar mitzvah. She never came back.

Poof; boom; goodbye, Mom.

Roberta felt bad for her father. He had to endure at least two or three weeks of limp string beans and overripe chopped liver before falling in love with another woman. She became Roberta's stepmother. She accepted the mantle of responsibility for the cooking, the cleaning, the driving, and, of course, the buying of everything. She and Roberta's father moved to Florida and raised a whole new family.

Roberta's mother sent wonderful letters and tapes from all over the world. She invited Roberta to join her in Nepal and Kenya, in New South Wales and Ann Arbor. Roberta was too shy and repressed to go. Besides, she was supposed to be mad at her mother for running away like that.

"Why did you do it, Mom?" she asked, sitting around drinking gin the night before her marriage to Gary Glass. "Why did you run away like that?"

Roberta's mother puffed on her cigarillo and

hitched her faded denim overalls, thinking. "I did it," she said finally, "because I could not bear to spend another minute shopping."

■   □   ■

So the grown-up and safely married Roberta who followed Susan north from Battery Park that beautiful Tuesday morning had grown to think of shopping as a real scary experience. She considered herself very lucky to have a sister-in-law like Leslie Glass who ordered her clothes, and a personal computer who ordered her food.

The fact that this meant she did not get to wear or eat anything she liked did not bother her.

She was much more frightened that, if she had to enter some store to buy something, she would suddenly freak out and turn (poof; boom; goodbye, Mom) into a liberated woman and have to run away from home.

Susan had no such reservations.

She loved shopping.

She treated herself to a long browse among the vendors of Lower Broadway. The whole street was her boutique. She had $100 in her drum case at the Port Authority just in case she saw something she might actually want to come back and *pay* for, and even though she felt bad that Jimmy had left so soon, and even though she could still feel the heat of his hand on her thigh, she wasn't going to let that ruin her day.

"Come on, baby," yelled an enterprising salesman, "you need some socks, you need a watch, you need some beads, I got 'em here, they'll fit right in your pretty little belly button!"

Susan grinned and bopped onward. Roberta hurried to keep up with her, losing sight of her once in a while behind a pair of lovers in military jackets with medals, behind pretty punk teenagers swishing in djelabas and dashikis from a hundred exotic tribes.

Susan swam the crowd like a guerrilla. Roberta tripped over it like a klutz. But she hung in. A mammoth fat man with a sweaty blue shirt flapping blocked her view. When she finally got past him, she saw Susan, trying on a pair of sunglasses.

The handsome black street vendor said, "Try these, momma," and he put another pair on Susan. "I got a hat for you too, baby—beautiful, beautiful, right?" He held up a mirror so Susan could see herself. It was the kind of hat Roberta's mother wore when she was still a housewife, back in the fifties—black, flat, and zooped up a little in the back. "Come on, baby, I got some jewelry here!" the vendor cooed. "Check it out!"

But Susan shook her head and moved on, past necklaces of plastic acorns, past plastic leopards with jeweled collars you could hang from your ears, past wind-up robots that marched in circles on the curb and had bees on their antennae. Susan smiled and almost glanced behind her, feeling . . . something . . . but then it turned out to be a skinny Frenchwoman with a silk tie and an apostrophe on her head. Susan just bopped on.

Roberta ducked out from behind the apostrophe where she had been hiding, and the handsome black vendor stopped her. He tried the sunglasses on her;

he plopped the hat on her head. "Now, this hat is gonna look great on you, lady," he said. "All day long I been trying to sell this hat." He held up the mirror. "Ten bucks," he said, "ten bucks for the set." Roberta grinned; she actually liked the hat. But then she saw Susan disappearing into the crowd and she took off, figuring if she lost her once she would never find her again.

"Hey, where you going with my hat?" the vendor yelled. "You come back here, give me my glasses . . ." Roberta ran back to return his stuff, crying, "Oh, I didn't mean . . . I'm sorry, I'm sorry," and she stumbled into his table and knocked everything—the glasses, the hats, the earrings, the beads, the wallets, the socks, the pirated tapes in pink plastic cases—all over the sidewalk.

"Oh Jesus, now what you doing, babe!" yelled the vendor. Roberta was running backward into the crowd, calling, "I'm sorry, sorry," but leaving him high and dry with the mess.

"Some of these broads you meet on the streets of New York . . ." he muttered to his buddies.

Susan had not noticed any of the commotion to her rear. She passed a gypsy palm reader telling the fortune of a Wall Street banker with an alligator attaché case. She passed a girl vendor with six pretty white rabbits, each one wearing twenty pairs of earrings. She passed a display of buttons hung on a low-floating kite. One of them said: "I've Got the Hots for Wilson Goode."

She trailed her fingers over Strawberry Shortcake bikini briefs and headsets left over from the Lufthansa heist and stacks of alligator patches you could sew on your clothes and a rack of glittery old Rockette costumes that hung outside a store called Love Saves the Day.

There she stopped.

Twenty feet behind her, Roberta stopped, panting. She was trying to figure out how Susan had learned to walk faster than Roberta could run.

Susan looked deeply into the store window.

It emitted a pink glow.

In it there was a pair of black boots, studded all over with chunky rhinestones. The boots were stuffed with pink tissue paper. They stood alone in the window.

Susan licked her upper lip. Roberta bit her lower lip. Was *this* what Susan wanted? Was *this* what Susan needed?

Roberta watched Susan enter the store. She was talking to the manager, a tall black man who looked exactly like Tina Turner. While Susan tried on the rhinestone-studded boots, Roberta slipped into Love Saves the Day. The little store bounced resoundingly with an Aretha Franklin tune. The wonderful junk dresses on multicolored hangers swung to the music. Roberta pretended to be very taken with one jazzy number.

Susan walked in the boots. She danced in them. She took off in them, smooth and fast as a magician's assistant.

But "Tina" was street-wise and broad-wise and not about to be fooled by Susan's sleight of foot. With Globetrotter hands, he drew Susan back into Love Saves the Day.

"Do me a favor, baby, stay on the carpet, okay?"

Groping among the clothes like an oaf, Roberta

could see that Susan would have to negotiate for the boots. The tension in the little pink boutique mounted.

"They're great, aren't they?" Susan said.

"Sure are," said the store owner.

"I gotta have 'em, man, but sixty-five bucks . . . ?"

"That is the price," he said, smoothing his fabulous blonde mop.

"Forget it," Susan said.

"I like your jacket," said the store owner.

Susan stayed cool.

"It used to belong to Jimi Hendrix," she said, very hesitant, as though she were afraid that Jimi might object.

Really she was reluctant to give up her pyramid jacket, which Jimmy Riddle had won for her in a Scrabble game against the head of women's wardrobe on a movie that ran out of money in Juárez, Mexico.

Juárez had never seen such a Scrabble game. Quarts of tequila flowed; sunrises came and went and came again. Dry Bones backed up Jimmy; the movie crew backed up women's wardrobe. The catering trailers fed everybody until the food ran out. The head of women's wardrobe began to starve. Jimmy survived because Susan sat at his feet and fed him stolen tacos. The Scrabble game took so long that by the time Jimmy finally won, the movie had been re-funded. The production manager arrived from LA, took everybody out for dinner, and flew the whole crew home in style. (Unfortunately, this airlift had occurred *after* the sets, the costumes, the sound equipment, and the grip stands had been sold to anyone who would pay cash, because no American movie crew wants to be stranded in Juárez without a per diem.)

Susan was very devoted to the pyramid jacket. It was a winning, given freely, proof of the only true love she had ever known. When she wore the jacket, she felt that no matter what was coming down, Jimmy Riddle was protecting her.

But that was just dumb, wasn't it? She didn't need protection. She could take care of herself. "I bet Jimmy would love it if I swapped the jacket for those boots," she said to the owner of Love Saves the Day.

He thought she meant Jimi Hendrix. "Deal," he said.

Roberta was so knocked out by the swiftness of this transaction that she knocked over the clothes she was pretending to look at and almost hung herself on a hanger. Before she could recover, Susan was gone.

Roberta ran to the doorway, looking up and down the street.

Susan had vanished.

She glanced over at the pyramid jacket, which the boutique owner was now hanging up with the rest of his rockabilly memorabilia.

"It's gorgeous, isn't it?" he said, taking in her white blouse and pink sweater. "Used to belong to Elvis Presley. You want to try it on?"

"All right," said Roberta timidly. It fit her perfectly. She had enough cash to pay for it, and the feel of the lapels made her tingle. For the first time in her life, Roberta Glass had gone shopping and actually bought something she liked.

■   □   ■

Roberta raced into the kitchen, wearing the pyramid jacket which she was sure Gary would love. Already it had helped make her less invisible in Fort Lee. When she stopped at the cleaner's to pick up Gary's suits, the counter-man had said, "Hey, some funky jacket, Mrs., uh . . . Mrs., uh . . ."

"Glass," Roberta said.

"Of course, how could I forget?" And he smiled at her.

She rushed to make that part of the dinner that Daisy the great maid had not made. The chicken was already turning on its spit. The coffee was already brewing on its timer. The salad was already crisping in the fridge. All Roberta had to do was whip up the quiche, one of Gary's favorites.

She punched a button on the VCR. Julia Child came on and told her to crack six eggs, two at a time, which of course a busy housewife could do before she left home in the morning, if only the housewife could *remember* to do this and not be a dumb-dumb who leaves it all for the last minute.

Gary arrived.

"Hello, Roberta," he said, kissing her on the cheek. "Hello, Julia. I am sorry, girls, but I can't stay for dinner. Some guy from Germany has fifteen hundred hot tubs waiting for me on a boat, and it turns out he cannot get them through customs with-out my connections. So I've got to have dinner with him in town." He knotted his tie, caught his reflection in the brilliant bottom of a polished pot, and smoothed his hair. Roberta sagged over her six eggs, beaten.

"It just happened," Gary explained. "I'm sorry." He bent to look into her lowered face as if she were a little girl, tilting her chiseled chin upward. "You forgive me?"

Roberta shrugged and began to grate an onion. Maybe at least he would notice the jacket.

"Did you get a good deal on the radio?" Gary asked.

The radio! The eight-speaker Dolby XBD equalizing floor-mounted goddamn radio! "Oh my God . . ." Roberta whispered, tears of shame and onion glazing her large blue eyes.

"You forgot the radio? Didn't you just come from the city?"

She shook her head, miserable and guilty.

When Gary Glass was disappointed, he had a way of staring at you uncomprehendingly and letting his mouth hang open like a whipped dog's. Either it touched your heart or it pissed you off.

"You know, Gary," Roberta snapped, imitating her sister-in-law, Leslie, "you could have *told* me about not wanting dinner instead of making me *rush!*"

"Rush?" he cried. "From where? According to you, you didn't go anywhere!" Suddenly he squinted at her. "What are you wearing?"

"It's a jacket," Roberta answered proudly. "It used to belong to Jimi Hendrix."

"You bought a *used* jacket? What are we, *poor?* What's going on here?"

She looked so utterly deflated that Gary was punched softly by remorse.

"Robertaaaaa, Robertaaaa," he said. "Now look, I've got to run, I'm late. We'll talk later, all right? All right? We'll talk later?" He kissed her on the cheek. He was afraid she was going to cry and make him late for his dinner appointment, so he stroked the idiotic black-and-gold-striped lapel of her jacket and tried to say something encouraging. "Jimi Hendrix, huh?"

Roberta was ready to throw the damn jacket in the trash compactor! She was ready to despoil the bright pink Love Saves the Day shopping bag with wet egg shells and onion skins! What a bust! What a total, unmitigated, infuriating failure! Once again Gary had looked at her and talked to her and kissed her, but he had not seen her once during this whole horrendous episode in the kitchen!

She hated this kitchen! She hated quiche! She hated Julia Child, and she hated her mother!

However, because Roberta did not do violent things, she folded up the pink shopping bag and put it in the drawer she reserved especially for that purpose. She threw the jacket, but not into the trash compactor, only over the back of a chair.

Out fell an odd-looking silver key with a red top, a piece of newspaper with someone's phone number written on it, and a Polaroid picture of Susan putting on her sexiest face. The key and number meant nothing to Roberta, so she just put them back in the jacket. But the picture, oh, the red-lipped picture, it caught her imagination and returned her like magic to her great day trailing Susan on the boutique street.

She studied the picture in her nice, luxurious bubble bath. She slipped beneath the perfumed waters. Fantastic ideas came into her head. The very next morning Roberta went back to New York and put an ad in The Personals of the New York *Mirror:*

Desperately seeking Susan, it said. *Meet me at Battery Park, Thursday 4:00 P.M.—regarding key.* And she signed it: *A Stranger.*

Meanwhile, Susan herself had doubled back to Love Saves the Day as soon as she realized she had left the Port Authority locker key in her pyramid jacket. But "Tina Turner" told her he had sold the jacket.

"In twenty minutes!"

"Sorry, babe," he said, throwing up his hands help-lessly.

Susan was beside herself. "I mean, what am I supposed to wear?" she raged to the sympathetic Crystal. She had left Crystal's number with "Tina." But actually she had little hope that the person who had bought her pyramid jacket would bring back the key.

Which was why she was so thrilled and ecstatic on Thursday morning upon reading Roberta's ad in The Personals.

"Great going, Stranger!" she beamed.

"What fucking stranger?" Jimmy Riddle exclaimed to no one in particular in Buffalo.

■ □ ■

Wayne Nolan walked out of that hotel in Atlantic City by the front door. He tried to look nondescript. He tried to keep his shoes quiet and his hands in his pockets so Bruce Meeker's blood wouldn't show. He figured he had between five and fifteen minutes to make his escape.

Bruce Meeker, Wayne's ex-partner, had not yet

fallen from the hotel-room window, but he was already dead, shot once by a gun equipped with a silencer. Wayne had propped the body on the window sill, estimating that there would be just enough time to get away before a breeze from the Atlantic tipped Bruce over the edge and onto the boardwalk below.

As it turned out, calm weather kept Bruce in place longer than Wayne had anticipated. The body didn't fall until Wayne was far away from the scene of the crime, driving on a cool, pleasant road through the Pine Barrens.

Wayne rented a room with a television in an ordinary motel and took a couple of Valiums. He sat on the bed with his panda bear. He tried to think clearly.

He had to find the girl he had passed on his way to Room 1313, the girl whose ghoulish satchel had opened in the hall, spilling her stuff outside the elevator. She must have the earrings. Wayne had ransacked Bruce's room, looking for the earrings, and Wayne was a very good ransacker. The earrings were nowhere to be found. The girl must have them.

"I swear to you, Wayne, baby." Bruce had insisted, "On my mother's grave I swear to you, I didn't give the earrings to Susan."

"Then why aren't they here?" Wayne asked softly. He rarely spoke above a mumble, a habit dictated by long experience in burglary.

"Maybe she stole them," Bruce suggested.

"You never spent the night with a woman who had the wit to steal anything," Wayne said.

"No, no, she's smarter than she looks," cried Bruce. He was naked in the bed, huddled under the sheets, and he was sweating. In all the years of their association, he had never seen his shifty, humorless partner holding a gun, and he did not fail to notice that Wayne's hands were trembling.

"For Chrissakes, put the gun away, Wayne, baby," he pleaded. "You didn't kill anybody in your whole career. You don't want a murder on your conscience now that you're about to become a father. Take it easy, cool down. . . ."

Bruce lunged up from the bed and kicked Wayne in the mouth—and Bruce had legs like Arnold Schwarzenegger. The gun went flying, landing under the drapes. Wayne dived for it, spitting out four of his back teeth. Bruce got there first.

He snatched the gun and aimed it at Wayne's blond head, but he had the disadvantage of being naked. Wayne grabbed his balls and squeezed—and Wayne had hands like Captain Lou Albano.

Bruce screamed. Wayne stifled his scream by stuffing the drapes in his mouth. Bruce twisted the gun around and prepared to shoot Wayne through the heart. Wayne broke Bruce's wrist. The gun went off.

Bruce Meeker died from the impact of one bullet that tore through his lower jaw and continued upward into his brain.

The drapes were drenched with blood. Wayne Nolan got a couple of spots on his tie and some more on his hands when he moved the body. But his tie, like his shirt and suit, were black, or almost black, so no one noticed the blood when he walked out of the hotel.

Clutching his panda, waiting for the Valium to work, Wayne stretched out on the motel bed. He tried doing the breathing exercises that he had learned in a childbirth-training class with his sweet wife in Marseilles. This partially controlled the pain in his jaw where his teeth had once been. Wayne figured the police would find his teeth in the hotel room. Teeth were a dead giveaway. In three days, six days maximum, every cop in the metropolitan area would have his dental records.

Interpol would be alerted. Inspector Eugene Licker would come flying in from Zurich. Wayne could just picture Licker's twisted little smile, his freckled bald head shiny with excitement. He had been pursuing Wayne Nolan for years, and this would be his big chance at the kill.

It was imperative that Wayne find the girl with the earrings before Licker found him.

He had only two clues to her whereabouts. On the room-service tray, he had discovered a newspaper with the first *Desperately seeking Susan* ad encircled by a black valentine. In addition, he had a snapshot of Susan—Bruce must have taken it—in white lace tights and short shorts. The picture gave Wayne a clear record of the pyramid jacket, which he would never have forgotten in any case, but really it focused on her behind. Bruce Meeker had always been a sucker for a well-shaped rear.

The Valium began to take effect. The blood in Wayne's mouth began to clot. He felt a little less upset now.

If only Bruce had been able to produce the earrings, Wayne would not have threatened him with the gun. But he was so mad at Bruce for stealing the earrings. It was such a lousy, rotten thing to do to an old friend. It showed Wayne that Mr. Baloney was right all along when he said, "Watch yourself, Wayne, my boy. This Bruce Meeker may be fast on his feet, but he won't make a good jewel thief in the end of days. He likes women too much. And thieves who like women too much are always giving things away. Your things, Wayne, my boy. *My* things."

Wouldn't you know that after all the planning and plotting and patience it took to steal a treasure in Egyptian artifacts from the Brooklyn Museum (the newspapers were already calling it the Great Queen of Egypt Caper), Bruce had done just what Mr. Baloney had predicted and made off with the priceless Nefertiti earrings and given them to some ditsy fluffhead who had now skipped to New York to meet some guy named Jim.

Wayne watched a rerun of "The Electric Company." He put some polish on the paw of his panda and polished his shoes. They were very expensive, orthopedically specialized shoes, and in their way they symbolized Wayne Nolan's long, troubled relationship with Bruce Meeker.

Many years before, when Wayne was just starting out as an apprentice thief with Mr. Baloney, he teamed up with a clumsy oaf who specialized in great art. They were assigned to dress up as delivery men and carry a large Fragonard out of a gallery on the French Riviera. Well, wouldn't you know, the clumsy oaf dropped his end of the Fragonard right on Wayne's toes.

So Wayne had all these broken toes and could not walk.

So what good is a professional thief who cannot walk?

It was lucky Mr. Baloney carried disability for his henchmen.

The clumsy oaf disappeared, never to be seen again—this was Mr. Baloney's get-well present to Wayne, his favorite apprentice, clearly a talented boy.

But the problem remained. Even when Wayne was up and about, exercising in the sunny Marseilles apartment where he and his nice French wife lived, it was clear that his toes would never be the same. He shuffled and staggered; every step he took made noise. He still had the best hands in the business and a special tenderness toward locks, but he needed a partner with swift, silent feet. "Someone who can get the most out of a gas pedal," he said softly to Mr. Baloney, "and run like hell."

The solution was Bruce Meeker.

A former film stunt man, Bruce could make a living only by leaping from burning buildings and driving across rivers without bridges. He had been drummed out of his IA local for trading a stolen grip stand for hash instead of cash in Juárez. So he had a healthy grudge against the establishment.

Physically, Bruce made a perfect partner for Wayne. But they had serious stylistic and emotional differences. Wayne was steady, conservative, and married, and Bruce was mercurial, flamboyant, and an incorrigible woman chaser. Wayne wore baggy black suits, black shirts, black ties, his special black-and-gray orthopedic shoes and, on moonlit nights, a black ski helmet to cover his blond hair. Bruce wore gold chains, custom-made silk suits, and flowered shorts.

Bruce gambled; Wayne saved. Bruce wanted to have sex; Wayne wanted to have babies.

Once, when they were posing as oil men at a fancy party in Kuwait, Bruce had been so overcome with emotion upon viewing the charms of some sheik's mistress that he forgot, he actually *forgot* that he and his partner, Wayne, had come to the party to steal the jewels of the host.

Imagine Wayne in the master bedroom, deftly defusing the ticking time bomb that guards the safe, meticulously dismantling the electronic circuitry that surrounds the lock, delicately undoing the snaps and buttons that guard the burglar alarm, finally lifting the naked gems from their velvet boxes. He has maybe twenty seconds to make it through the window, climb down the bougainvillea vines, and slip into the getaway car, which Bruce is driving. Imagine Wayne's distress when he finds no Bruce, no getaway car, nothing but forty miles of trackless desert between himself and the Persian Gulf!

Luckily a caravan came by, and Wayne hitched a ride on a camel. The gems were stuffed painfully in his orthopedic shoes. He looked back once and saw, with satisfaction, Bruce Meeker running from the house, trying to hold his pants up while fierce men in white robes chased him, brandishing daggers.

The episode ended successfully enough. Wayne made it to the launch that was waiting for him in the harbor, tore off his shoes, and sped away to Egypt. In Cairo, he had a nice wife with downcast eyes. She comforted him and rubbed his feet. Mr. Baloney fenced the Kuwaiti jewels and gave Wayne Bruce's cut.

One day, Wayne went to the Cairo Museum to wander among the artifacts. What pretty things some of these queens of ancient Egypt had! What a lot of diamonds and emeralds and gold and rubies they embedded in their bangle bracelets! In strolled Bruce Meeker.

"Did your wife tell you I came by looking for you?" Bruce said.

"I was hoping you were dead."

"She's a lovely girl."

"You're an asshole, Meeker. Get out of my sight."

"Listen, Wayne, baby, I'm sorry, okay? I'm sorry. I just got sidetracked by that broad at the party in Kuwait and the precise time escaped me."

"You know how many agonizing hours I spent at the podiatrist after that caper?"

"Please, Wayne, please take me back. I've got the best idea, but I can't pull it off without your golden hands."

"I don't want to hear it," Wayne said, shuffling and squeaking off into the mummy room.

Bruce was right behind him. "In six months the whole collection of royal jewels you were just admiring is going to be shipped to Brooklyn as part of a massive American-Egyptian cultural exchange," he said.

"Keep your voice down, minibrain," Wayne said.

"It's all going into crates, and the crates are gonna have special customized locks, and last night in a gin game in Aswan, I severely defeated the guy who makes the locks."

Wayne felt his toes itching. That meant they were healing.

"Can he be bought?" Wayne asked.

"For a mere fraction of what he lost to me in that gin game," said Bruce, grinning.

No sooner had Wayne and Bruce made friends again when, wouldn't you know, Inspector Eugene Licker of Interpol, Swiss by origin and temperament, ran into the mummy room and arrested Wayne. There ensued a major legal battle over who should have the right to prosecute. The Kuwaiti government wanted Wayne returned to the host whose jewels he had heisted so his left hand could be cut off. The French government, which had been forced to buy back the Fragonard from those who had bought it from those who had bought it from those who had bought it from Mr. Baloney, wanted Wayne so his head could be cut off. The Italian government wanted Wayne so that they could grant him immunity in exchange for information about Mr. Baloney.

Therefore, Wayne fled to Jamaica, where he had a nice wife. She kept herself busy in his absence by weaving baskets and stringing seeds. She sang lilting songs, like a yellow bird.

Mr. Baloney's brilliant lawyers saw to it that almost all the cases against Wayne alone were locked up in paperwork for many years. The one bit of legal amnesia they could *not* arrange concerned a small caper Bruce and Wayne had pulled smuggling diamonds into Miami in Cabbage Patch dolls. The diamonds were minor. They belonged to some wealthy lady Bruce had seduced in Rio. But Wayne should never have lifted that shipment of Cabbage Patch dolls. Because every time a customs official had to cut into the heart of a doll to retrieve a diamond, some real little girl's heart broke in two.

So Bruce and Wayne were convicted on the lesser charge of smuggling recovered goods. However, they never went to prison. First they posted bail; then they appealed the bail; then they won the appeal, settled the bail, and appealed the conviction. Pending that appeal, they began meeting secretly again in Brooklyn, to plan the Great Queen of Egypt Caper.

Wayne had no wife in Brooklyn.

This made him lonely and irritable.

The hard pavements of the city beat up his toes.

Bruce introduced him to women, but none of them were nice.

The caper was a week away, and there was nothing to do but wait.

On orders from Mr. Baloney, Bruce raced around Central Park mile after grueling mile, which was how he got thighs like Arnold Schwarzenegger.

Wayne was spotted lurking near a Toys-for-Boys outlet. Baloney cracked down right away. "I want Wayne Nolan stashed in a safe place!" he bellowed at his lawyers. "Away from temptation!"

The brilliant lawyers set Wayne up as a night watchman in a day-care center for very intelligent children. All the toys there were made of solid blond wood and bored Wayne. The day-care authorities accepted him happily after doing a thorough check and finding that, although he was a famous international jewel thief, he was extremely neat in his personal habits and had no record of child abuse.

Finally, the great moment came. Their watches synchronized, their blood racing, Wayne Nolan and Bruce Meeker closed in on the Brooklyn Museum.

It was a dark and stormy night. The entire museum security staff was occupied trying to contain a massive demonstration against the mounting of a highly publicized show of erotic quilts. Crowds of fundamentalists and feminists encircled the museum crying, "Keep your dirty blankets off our children!" Meanwhile, in the basement, Bruce Meeker locked his powerful legs around a rafter and hung upside down while Wayne Nolan, who had opened the crates with the Aswan passkey, passed up to him priceless necklaces of crystal acorns, a matched pair of ebony leopards with jeweled collars, and ancient talismans that said, "Pharaoh eats dung."

And earrings. Lots of earrings. One pair of earrings in particular that had belonged to Queen Nefertiti herself and carried little cameos of her face surrounded by gold and hammered brass and blue crystal. The items were small, but together their street value ran into the tens of millions.

Bruce and Wayne hastily camouflaged the hole in the basement ceiling through which they had entered the crate room and hurried out into the seething and angry streets. The demonstrating crowds absorbed them instantly. And the theft was not discovered until the next morning, when an exhausted security man plunged through the hole, his fall broken only by the intervention of an erotic quilt.

By that time Wayne Nolan had dutifully delivered the whole haul to Mr. Baloney. Baloney was thrilled. He loved artifacts. There was only one trouble. Bruce Meeker had pocketed the Nefertiti earrings and skipped town.

Wayne burst into tears. This time the tension had really gotten to him. His poor toes had been stepped on by a formidable political coalition! He wanted his panda! He wanted to go straight! He wanted to go home to his wives, all of whom were now pregnant, and play with his babies!

"Not just yet, my boy," said Mr. Baloney. "You were the one who took Bruce Meeker back. You're the one who's got to get my earrings back. That's only fair, don't you think?"

Wayne fell asleep in his Pine Barrens motel. Soon he would become the third person in New York to be desperately seeking Susan.

All day Wednesday he scanned The Personals looking for a clue to the destination of the girl with the pyramid jacket. On Thursday morning he bought another newspaper. Sure enough, the ad was there. *Four P.M.*, it said. *The Battery.*

Wayne drove his car into a swamp, stole somebody's Chevy, and headed for New York. His panda sat beside him, in the passenger seat, and in the panda's belly was the stubby black gun.

■　□　■

Upon reading Roberta's "Stranger" ad in Buffalo, Jim Riddle called his best friend, Dezmund O'Herlihy. Jim called from a pay booth. He reached Dez in a projection booth. The last thing Dez needed was this phone call.

Today was his day to earn an honest living and stay out of trouble. Today he had concluded, after much soul-searching, that he really preferred the quiet life of meditation and contemplation and the steady pursuit of his ambition, which was to be a highly regarded independent filmmaker.

He no longer wanted to discuss his secret ambition,

which was to be the king of Hollywood—no, no, that was all behind him now—he had grown up; he had accepted his limitations and was enjoying his (rather dark but safe) niche above the audience at the Bleecker Street Cinema.

On Thursday at three o'clock, when his best friend, Jim, called, Dez was projecting *Mutant Rage*, one of the greats in the splatter genre. Dez noted the now-classic combination of slow motion and a wobbly dolly that made the cannibalism sequence so unsteadying. He murmured his admiration at the powdery white light created by deliberate overexposure every time the main character threw up. These observations served to distract Dez and strengthen his resolve not to think about the rest of his life, which was in the toilet.

Then Jim called.

"Can you hear me, Dez?" screamed Jimmy.

"Why are you screaming?" Dez answered calmly.

"I'm in Buffalo!" Jim screamed.

"Oh, of course. Now I understand," said Dez.

He thought that Jim must be at a zoo because there was so much squawking in the background. Unbeknown to Dez, the squawking came from Mitzi, chief chick in the Dry Bones entourage, who had just been told that the Buffalo concert included festival seating. "And festival seating means Port-O-Sans!" she squawked, "and Port-O-Sans mean pissing with flies! I am not gonna piss with flies! You guys can piss in bottles! What the hell is this, Woodstock?"

"I'm trying to talk to somebody in New York here, Mitzi!" Jim yelled at her. "Hold it down, will you?"

"Hold on a minute," Dez said to him from New

York. The big battle scene between the Mutants and the Earthmen was reaching its climax, and so was the reel, which had to be changed immediately. Dez tucked the phone under his ear, trying to jiggle the celluloid into place.

"I've got a problem," Jim yelled to him.

So did Dez. The reel had run out. The audience began to scream and riot.

"I need a favor," Jim was saying. "It's about Susan."

"Boo, hiss," went the audience. Soon they were clapping rhythmically. Dez remained calm and completely in control.

"Move your ass up there!" screamed the audience, while Jim told this crazy story about his crazy girlfriend, Susan, being mixed up in a murder and some guy named Stranger who was sending her messages in The Personals. "She's supposed to meet him at four o'clock!" Jim yelled.

"Just give me a chance, folks," Dez said nicely to the audience, sticking his head out of the booth window.

"Just do me a favor and go down to the Battery and see that she's okay—okay, Dez?"

"I've got a job here, you know, Jim. . . ."

"Come on, Dez. It'll take you half an hour."

"How long is it gonna take you to change the reel, asshole?" screamed the audience.

"Even if I could get someone to fill in for me, I still don't know what Susan looks like," Dez said. He finally had the reel in place, but now the projector was stalling.

"Schmuck!" yelled the audience.

"You said it," Dez muttered to himself, because

within an hour he had cajoled a friend into replacing him in the projection booth, borrowed a motor scooter, and was cruising down Broadway toward the Battery looking for Susan.

Dez O'Herlihy could not understand at this moment how decent, hard-working, intelligent men like himself and Jim Riddle got mixed up with these catastrophic broads. His own girl, Victoria, had sailed out of his life last night as suavely as a schooner.

"It's over, Dezmund," she said. "I have had my fill of living as an East Village punk sculptress. I long for my roots. I am going back to the East Fifties."

It's over? Just like that, it's over? How about a little preamble maybe? Dez wondered. A couple of opening credits, perhaps an argument about something significant, a chronic complaint or two, some little *hint* that this relationship had lost its sprockets? But no, not with Victoria. She didn't believe in hints. She had to operate by thunderbolt, like Thor.

Calm yourself, he said to himself at a red light. It happens, right? Think positively. At least Victoria didn't steal anything on her way out—unlike the famous Susan, who, Dez had been told, stole pants and shirts and headsets and front doors, and, most humiliating of all, the good sense of a great guy like Jimmy. Jimmy had said on the phone from the zoo, "She's incredibly pretty. Blonde hair, medium height, a green-and-gold jacket with a pyramid with an eye on top like a dollar bill—you can't miss it."

Dez sighed. A barreling taxi almost killed him. He swerved agreeably out of the way. He thought maybe he should take an aggressiveness-training course.

In the barreling taxi, Susan herself was having a

difficult time. Her lipstick had smeared. A little red tributary trickled down from the corner of her mouth, and she dabbed at it patiently, but she couldn't get it to leave. Meanwhile, the creep who was driving the cab would not shut up. "I lived in New York all my life," he said. "We used to have Chinese restaurants, Italian restaurants. Now you have these sushi restaurants. Everyone goes for sushi, sushi. I hate the stuff."

This cab driver then almost killed a guy on a motor scooter who was wearing a red helmet that said "Dragon Noodle" on it, giving Susan a start and making her *once again* smear the lipstick she had finally fixed. "Although, I tell you," he said, not noticing that Susan was about to cry. "I had some the other day. I took it home, cooked it. It wasn't bad. Tasted like fish."

Roberta was already at the Battery. She leaned against the railing where Jim and Susan had kissed so passionately, displaying the back of her pyramid jacket, by which she expected Susan to recognize her. She had fixed her hair like Susan's, in wild, kinky waves, she had bought some light-purple pants and red boots and a jeweled satchel pocketbook at a store her sister-in-law, Leslie, was never likely to enter. She felt that she looked terrific and couldn't wait to see whether Susan would recognize her as a kindred spirit. Maybe they would be able to have a drink together. Maybe dinner. Maybe Susan would take her to a disco and introduce her to her friends. Maybe she would meet a friend of Jim's . . . a musician maybe, or a roadie who does lights for rock concerts. Roberta was so excited at the prospect of meeting the kind of men Susan might know that her feet began to sweat.

Wouldn't you know, a weird blond guy in a black suit with a black shirt shuffled up to her and said, "Hi. You look like I've seen you somewhere before."

Roberta felt sick.

He had a smile like a limp string bean.

"I don't think we've met before," she said, leaning away from him.

"Yeah, I think so," he answered.

He stepped closer. Oh my God, she thought, where the hell is Susan?

"You doing anything right now?" asked the man, peeking stealthily under his own ear.

"I'm waiting for someone," Roberta answered.

He ran his pale, slightly golden fingers over Roberta's jacket sleeve. Her skin crawled. More and more frantic, she searched the Battery with her eyes, desperate to spot Susan. But Susan was nowhere to be found. She might have missed the ad, God forbid. She might have had second thoughts and gone off to join Jimmy. Roberta had to get away from this overbearing weirdo whose breath was messing up her hair, but if she got too far away, Susan might miss her!

Susan! she prayed. Please show up *now!*

The taxi containing the answer to Roberta's prayers bumped to a halt. "That'll be nine-twenty," said the driver. Susan gave him some quarters and said, "Keep the change" and waltzed off, looking for her Stranger.

It was Susan's first miscalculation since she tried to rip off "Tina Turner" at Love Saves the Day. The street-wise broad-wise cab driver immediately flagged down a cop, who immediately arrested Susan.

"You don't understand!" Susan yelled, twisting in the arms of the law. "I have to meet someone here."

"We'll talk about it in the car," said the cop.

"There she is!" Susan protested, for she had spotted Roberta in her jacket. "She's got all my stuff! She'll give you the goddamn cab fare!"

The policeman placed Susan firmly in his car just as Roberta gave up and hurried away from her place at the railing, trying to shake the blond guy with the shifty gait who would not leave her alone.

Wayne stuck to her like pantyhose. She bit her fingernails, giving in to panic. Meanwhile, Susan went to jail.

"Do you like candy?" Wayne asked softly. "I've got some Sugar Babies here."

"No, thank you," Roberta answered.

"Um, well, uh, I wanted to say, why don't we have a chat, because I was very close to your boyfriend in Atlantic City. Well, not exactly close to him, but you know . . ."

"No, no, no!" Roberta said. "I'm married."

"Oh, I don't think so." Wayne laughed. "No, I do not think so." He took her arm. She pulled it away. She changed direction. So did he. He grabbed her by the armpit. He had hands like iron. "Did your boyfriend make you wear the pretty little earrings he gave you? Why don't we have a chat about that, because my car is just over there. . . ."

"Let go of me!" Roberta yelled. Her throat was closing; her legs were collapsing. She wanted to scream.

"Susan!" Dez O'Herlihy called, spotting the pyramid jacket.

"Let go of me!" she screamed at Wayne Nolan, struggling to get away from him. From out of nowhere came this guy on a blue motor scooter, calling "Susan!" and riding straight at them. Wayne took one look at the menacing red Dragon Noodle helmet and released Roberta. She ran screaming into something hard and knocked herself unconscious.

Into the gray, choppy seas rolled the brand-new pocketbook containing all her identification.

And Roberta Glass, who had never possessed a very clear idea of who she was to begin with, now lost consciousness and with it any recollection of her former self.

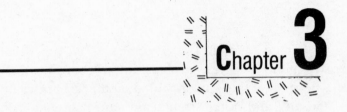
Roberta woke up.

For some reason she was lying on her back on a sidewalk.

An angel was hovering above her. He had a glow around his face. He had bluebirds in his eyes.

She blinked.

The glow around the angel's head shimmered away. She could see that he had a wide mouth and a longish nose and a day's growth, that for some reason he was wearing overalls and appeared worried about her.

"Susan?" he said.

Ah, her name was Susan. And this beautiful guy who smelled of spareribs must be her lover, awakening her in the morning. They were free spirits. Maybe happy-go-lucky bag people. That's why they had slept on the sidewalk.

"What happened?" she asked.

"Are you okay?"

"My head hurts."

Her head hurt so much that she revised the whole scenario.

She was a trapeze artist, so courageous and daring that she never used a net. She had fallen out of the iron-strong hands of the man who was trying to catch her, and was expected to die. The circus-goers had gathered in close to mourn her passing. She could see their feet all around her. She could hear their murmurs of regret and distress.

Now, this kindly, concerned young man hovering above her was an off-duty clown; that's why he was wearing overalls. For years he had worshipped her from afar but always feared to tell her of his love because she had a partner who could kill you with his bare hands. So this was the very first time that she . . . what was her name? . . . ah yes, Susan . . . that she, Susan, was seeing the beautiful clown without his big red nose.

His eyes were deep-set, shadowed by low, shaggy brows and long lashes; like bluebirds, thought the fallen trapeze artist, like bluebirds in delicate cages.

"I'm Dez," he said. "I'm a friend of Jim's."

Roberta squeezed her eyes shut. "Who's Jim?" she asked. She tried to sit up, but she couldn't.

"Your boyfriend, Jim," said the young man. "Who was the guy hassling you?" He encircled her with long, worried arms. "Easy," he said, "easy," helping her to her feet.

"What guy?" she asked.

"The guy who just ran off."

"I don't know."

"You don't know?"

"I don't remember."

"You don't remember? Are you okay? You want to see a doctor?"

"No, I'm okay," she answered. Now that Roberta was standing and knew that she was *not* a trapeze artist who had missed her handoff and would soon die of injuries sustained in her fall, she felt better. Her head hurt less and less. So whose were the hands she recalled with so much fear? This guy who called himself Dez had large, comforting hands that steadied her as she tried to walk.

"You're okay," he said.

Well, if he said so . . .

"She's okay," he told the crowd. "Show's over. She's with me. She's okay."

He led Roberta to a park bench and sat her down. What bay was that over there? Were they on vacation maybe? Of course, that must be it. They were on vacation at the shore . . . the Jersey shore maybe. . . . She felt that once, long ago she . . . what was her name? . . . oh yes, Susan . . . may have been to the Jersey shore with people who called themselves Mom and Daddy . . . or the Costa del Sol. . . . Right, Susan was in Spain by the swank Mediterranean, and this guy's name was China or Porcelain. . . . No . . . that wasn't right. . . .

"Do you remember anything?" Dez asked.

"I don't know," she said.

"How'd you get here?"

"I don't know."

"Do you remember what you had for breakfast?"

Why did bagels occur to her? Maybe she was Jew-ish.

"I don't know."

"You are Susan, aren't you?"

"Susan?"

"You don't know?"

She shook her head.

He sighed.

"Okay," he said, "where's your purse?"

Roberta looked all over for it, but she found no purse.

Ah, well then, here was the answer to the mystery! If she had no purse, she must have been *hiking*.

"Okay, no purse," Dez said.

But no one went hiking in red boots.

"You got anything in your pockets?"

Roberta felt all over for pockets. She had only one, inside her jacket. It contained a key and a piece of newspaper.

"All right!" beamed Dez. "Now we're getting some-place. This is my phone number written here. Jim must have given it to you."

"Jim?"

"Jim, your boyfriend."

"Oh yeah, Jim. My boyfriend."

"Do you remember him?" Dez asked, hopefully.

"No."

Her head had now stopped hurting. Little visions were beginning to come to her—choppy seas, iron railings, hard benches, passionate kisses, a black man with blond hair, a blond man with black clothes—it was all very hazy, but . . . "This is like a déjà vu," she murmured.

"How can you have a déjà vu if you don't remember anything?" asked Dez.

Now he sounded annoyed, and Roberta decided she did not like him as much as she had originally.

"I simply feel like I have seen all of this before!" she said sharply. "But I have never seen you before, and I have never seen this key before in my entire life!"

She shoved a key with a red plastic cap into his large hands, which were very dirty anyway and really rather disgusting, just like his sparerib aftershave.

"This is a Port Authority locker key," he said. (Well, if he said so . . .) "All right. I'll tell you what I'm gonna do. I'm gonna run you up to the Port Authority. Maybe whatever is in the locker will help you snap out of it. How's that?"

For the first time, he smiled at Roberta.

A bluebird flew into her chest and flapped its wings disturbingly on the nether side of her rib cage.

"Let's go," Dez said, indicating his motor scooter. For some reason, he seemed to assume she was familiar with such things—in fact, she did not even know where to sit. Maybe she was supposed to sit in the basket in the front of the scooter that said "Dragon Noodle" and appeared to be designed for carrying takeout orders.

She followed him meekly, disturbed by the flapping of the damn bird.

Dez stopped short, his sweet, sensitive, rather artistic face suddenly twisted by paranoia (a hint—but who could know it then?—of how he would often look in the future when he finally became the king of Hollywood).

"Wait just one minute here," he said. "This isn't some sort of trick, is it? I mean, I know a little bit about you, Susan, okay? So don't even consider jerking me around, because I am not in a great mood today."

Roberta had heard this tone someplace before. . . . Had Aretha Franklin once used it in a song? Had the black man with the blond hair once used it in a store? Why was she—uh, what was her name? . . . uh . . . uh . . . *Susan!* Right!—a nice, innocent woman, maybe a little confused, generating so much suspicion? She did not even know what *jerk around* meant! It sounded disgusting and masturbatory!

"Why should I want to jerk you around?" she asked. "I mean, I don't even know you."

Dez sighed. He gave her the helmet to wear—all he needed was for her to bang her head again—and assumed she would climb on the scooter behind him. So she did.

But when Roberta locked her hands on his warm, hard belly, the bluebird went crazy and her hands began to melt. She tried not to press herself too closely against his back, seeing that he was a friend of this guy—what was his name? Oh yes, Jim—who was supposed to be her boyfriend. But she *had* to press against him to survive the bouncy ride to the Port Authority.

The scooter started out in the key of B-flat. As it warmed up, the pitch ascended to C. Traffic got thicker. They ducked by a bus. The crowds pressed closer. They raced a cab. Jackhammers drilled to the beat. The blue scooter sang in C-sharp, no less! And the singing started in the scooter's seat. Roberta shifted. But she couldn't escape. Big waves of music hummed in her crotch. They passed men at work. They leaped Con Ed. They missed three beats at a long red light, but the singing didn't stop. It turned on her jacket. It rolled through her helmet. Boy, this machine could sing high!

Good sound rises, said a voice from the past.

Roberta told herself that she was experiencing an audio phenomenon created by the vibrations of an overworked motor with a very old muffler.

But she knew better, and so did Dezmund O'Herlihy.

■   □   ■

Initially, Wayne Nolan figured that the loony on the motor scooter must be a member of some Shiite death squad subcontracted by Inspector Eugene Licker of Interpol. (Long experience told him that true believers usually work for money in the end.) Who else would ride in an unprotected vehicle directly into the face of a famous jewel thief who had (everyone would presume) already killed one person and must surely be armed and dangerous?

But then the loony let him get away. Didn't even pursue him as he shuffled and staggered through the crowd. And pursuit would have been easy, for Wayne's Sugar Baby bag was leaking and leaving a squooshed but quite legible trail.

Wayne ducked into a shadow. He tried to think clearly.

By now, he figured, his teeth had been identified. So Bruce Meeker's death was no mystery to the authorities any longer. But had they connected Meeker and Nolan to the Great Queen of Egypt Caper?

Wayne thought probably they had.

Not many teams in the world could have pulled off that stunt. Licker would consider Yoko and the Walrus—but they were in Surrey working the garden-party circuit. He would consider the Walker Clan. But they had already been hauled in for questioning in connection with the disappearance of American naval superiority.

So Licker would be forced to conclude that the culprits were Meeker and Nolan. He would contemplate Bruce's ransacked hotel room. He would conclude that something had been searched for there.

But would he know what it *was*?

Wayne didn't think so. No, Wayne thought not.

As an expert on the personality of Bruce Meeker, Inspector Licker might correctly assume that Bruce had swiped some item from the Brooklyn Museum heist. However, he could not know which item, could he? Mr. Baloney had the whole cache stashed far beyond the prying nose of the law; he would undoubtedly hold it unsold, its value escalating wildly, for a number of years, and then, when the New York police were bored with the search and Lloyds of London had long ago paid up and the Egyptian officials involved had been retired in disgrace, Baloney would leak the treasure, item by item, like bad news, reaping unconscionable profits.

So at this moment Inspector Licker could not know it was the Nefertiti earrings in particular that Wayne Nolan was looking for. He could only know that *if* he found Wayne Nolan.

Wayne smiled to himself.

As usual, he was just a couple of steps ahead of Interpol. He ran out of Sugar Babies so he bought a box of Dots and gnawed them on the good side of his mouth and headed for his car.

The car was being towed away, not because it was stolen, but because it was five minutes over on the meter. Thank God Wayne's panda was safely hidden at the day-care center.

Wayne hailed a taxi. This was always very hard for him to do because he never raised his voice. "Taxi," he mumbled, peeking under his own ear to see if anybody was listening. "Oh, taxi." Luckily a cab pulled up to drop off a girl with six rabbits that were wearing lots of earrings. Wayne slipped in. "Follow that scooter," he mumbled.

There was so much uptown traffic at five-thirty that the scooter carrying Dez and Roberta couldn't go very fast, and neither could the cab carrying Wayne. This gave Wayne time to gnaw his Dots and continue to refigure his situation.

The latest intelligence Wayne had on Licker's progress was a report from one of Mr. Baloney's couriers. The organization had checked the Zurich flights and found that, for the first time in Swiss history, they were all delayed. Apparently some rock star who wore her underwear as outerwear had arrived in Switzerland for a concert and had created such a commotion that the Swiss had actually lost track of the time. If Licker got word of Meeker's death on Monday, and today was Thursday, that meant Licker might still be stuck in Zurich.

But the idea of a stuck Licker was hard for Wayne to swallow.

He kept his shifty eyes on the blue motor scooter singing in C-sharp just ahead of his cab. He allowed himself a few moments of happiness, thinking about the little white and brown and black babies who would soon call him "Daddy."

Through his courier, Mr. Baloney had pointed out to Wayne one other fly in the ointment that must be quickly swatted.

The Nefertiti earrings themselves were now familiar to Americans because of television exposure. They had become the stars of the six-o'clock news. (Of course, all the artifacts stolen from the Brooklyn Museum were displayed and described, but it's hard to get the American public excited about pirated Viking Jew's harp music.)

"The earrings *play* better," explained Ted Koppel to the Egyptian ambassador right before the "Nightline" special on which the ambassador offered a $100,000 reward for the return of his nation's treasures. Onto every screen in America came an image of the gold and hammered brass and ancient blue glass jewels encasing cameo carvings of Nefertiti herself.

"I know my adopted country, Wayne, my boy," said Mr. Baloney. "At this very moment a thousand enterprising Americans are out in the garage smelting in the great tradition of Paul Revere. By the end of the week, a thousand brilliant fake Nefertiti earrings will be showing up at Egyptian diplomatic offices. Shortly thereafter, street vendors will be selling horrible reproductions for $2.50 each; they will swing from the ears of tacky women on street corners from Orlando to Davis. You'd better come up with the real thing fast, Wayne, my boy, before your task becomes immeasurably more complicated."

Dez and Roberta parked their scooter and entered the Port Authority Bus Terminal. Wayne left his taxi inching in the midtown gridlock. He found a doorway that offered him a clear view of the blue scooter and incidentally the white courtesy telephones clustered by the entrance to the massive terminal.

Not taking his keen, sneaky eyes off the scooter or the phones, Wayne made a call to Mr. Baloney.

"Hi," said the Baloney machine. "We're not in now. But leave a message and we'll call you if we ever return. Don't be sad; look on the bright side. Maybe *you* won't be in when *we* call, and we shall never have to speak to each other at all."

Wayne left a message after the beep.

Then he called the Port Authority.

"I want to request a page," he said softly.

"Speak up, please."

"A page."

"What?"

"I want to page someone."

"I'm afraid I can't understand what you are saying, sir or madam, as the case may be. Please call back when you are feeling stronger, or write a note and deliver it in person."

The Port Authority hung up.

Wayne wrote a note. He shuffled across the street and delivered it. Then he shuffled back to his doorway.

He watched to see whether anybody answered the page and came to the white courtesy telephones.

No one.

All clear.

So he collected some old shopping bags, bottles, and other debris, gathered it around him in the doorway, and settled back to wait and watch. Long experience told him that no New Yorker who is rushing to get home after a day's work is going to bother a derelict in a doorway, so he felt safe. But he also felt hungry, and that made him lonely for his wives, and loneliness is the mother of paranoia.

Wayne imagined that Roberta and Dez had entered the Port Authority and boarded a bus to someplace Wayne would never think of, taking the earrings with them and leaving the blue motor scooter behind as a red herring.

He imagined that the Baloney organization had abandoned him in this unpleasant city, had given up on the earrings and retired to their yacht off the Carolina coast.

He imagined that the guy selling *Muhammad Speaks* at the Port Authority entrance was an undercover cop sent by Abdul el Bul Bul, emir of police for the Sheikdom of Kuwait, waiting for one clear shot at Wayne's golden hands. He imagined that the blind man with the yellow cur groveling at his heels was really Inspector Rheum of the Paris police, waiting for one clear shot at Wayne's golden head.

Huddled in his doorway, he imagined everything but the truth.

The brilliant Swiss Inspector Eugene Licker of Interpol had made the most serious mistake of his career.

He had never come to New York.

Assuming that Wayne had retrieved some item(s)

from the Queen of Egypt Caper before killing Bruce Meeker, Licker had decided to circumvent the Zurich airport rock blockade by driving overland to Marseilles, then sailing to Cairo, then flying to Kingston, terrorizing Wayne's wives and ransacking their sunny apartments—and Licker was a very good ransacker.

Of course, he found nothing.

Licker should have known, as an expert on the personality of Wayne Nolan, that Wayne would not give a thing that belonged to Mr. Baloney to any wife of his.

But, in his blundering, Licker did manage to complicate Wayne's situation. For he revealed to three nice, innocent women that each was not, as she had previously thought, the one and only Mrs. Wayne Nolan.

Out of the Port Authority came Dez and Roberta. They had with them the same skull-patterned satchel Wayne had seen in Atlantic City. He grinned slightly in his shadow. Pay dirt.

A nondescript black car pulled up.

In it was one of Mr. Baloney's most trusted couriers.

"I know it's hard for you, Wayne, baby," she said, "but next time you leave a message on the machine, could you talk a little louder?"

She gave Wayne the car keys and slid out the passenger side and vanished. On the front seat of the car was a CARE package. It contained pliable foods that a man who had recently lost a lot of teeth might be able to handle—apple sauce, peanut-butter-and-jelly sandwiches, and Julia Child's creamiest quiche. Also a thermos of coffee and a whole stack of E-Man comics. Wayne's panda was there, too, and in his belly a message. "Don't go back to the day-care center," it said. "Every intelligent kid in America is looking for you."

Wayne felt wonderful.

All his suspicions had been groundless.

He liked this car. It didn't have itchy seat covers.

The satchel he wanted was heading downtown, bumping along on the motor scooter not two hundred feet in front of him. Sooner or later—and, he sincerely hoped, without further violence—he would have the earrings that must be inside, and he would be able to retire a rich man and return at last to the arms of his devoted wives.

■   □   ■

Roberta got very excited when the Port Authority locker opened and she saw the Dry Bones drum case. If it was hers, it sure was *chic!* "Oooh, I hope it's filled with something good," she whispered, like a little girl, Dez thought, like a little girl making a wish for her birthday.

Well, the satchel was filled with forks and knives, as well as clothes. A black merry-widow bra came out of it, embarrassing Roberta. Also saltwater taffy, black-rubber car parts, and every kind of crucifix imaginable. ("I must have been off base about the bagels," Roberta thought. "Clearly Susan is not Jewish.") There were Mexican silver earrings, Canadian fur earrings ("You sure do move around a lot," Dez commented), and one absolutely fabulous earring that looked not completely unfamiliar.

Roberta closed her eyes. "When I close my eyes I see a pyramid," she said.

"Like on your jacket?" Dez suggested.

"Oh yeah, that must be what it is."

Dez glanced at the watch he kept turned inward on his wrist. His downstairs neighbor Choy was waiting for the return of the motor scooter at the Dragon Noodle and by now would have been badly inconvenienced and extremely pissed.

"Okay, well, at least now you've got everything, Susan," he said. "I hope you're feeling better—you are feeling better, aren't you?"

"Oh yeah," she murmured vaguely, still engrossed in the big earring.

"Good. 'Cause I've got to get the scooter back. I'll see you around maybe sometime, okay? I'll see you with Jim."

"Who?"

"Good-bye, Susan."

"What?"

To Dez riding down the escalator, Jim's girl, Susan, looked as though she had just been pushed off a train into a desert. She sat with her legs straight out in front of her, the satchel's contents tumbled around her knees, her large, blue eyes alternately blank and tumultuous. Dez was really committed to leaving her there, really committed; he had already killed enough of his day baby-sitting this broad. But when he glanced back, she was lighting a cigarette, and she looked just as she had looked getting on the scooter, as though she had never done this thing ever before in her entire life.

"Eugene Licker," called the Port Authority PA system. "Eugene Licker, please pick up the white courtesy telephone."

The announcement jarred Dez. For some reason,

it sounded to him like an air-raid warning, triggering his alarm instinct and making up his mind. He knew this girl was not jerking him around! He knew she was sincerely amnesiac and totally out of it and that she was gonna sit there in front of the Port Authority lockers all night long! Brushing past commuters, he ran up the down escalator.

"Okay, Susan," he said, "you can sleep at my place. One night. One night only. On the couch." He re-packed her suitcase. She was trying to figure out how to use the lighter. "But I don't want any drama, I don't want any of your friends coming over, and I want nothing disappearing from my apartment, you got that?"

Roberta finally had the cigarette lit. She inhaled. A fit of coughing rendered her unable to respond.

"Maybe you should quit," Dez said and took her home with him.

He could not believe, with all he knew about Susan, that he had actually *fallen* for the amnesia ploy. He could not believe Jim's notorious girl had actually convinced him that she did not know how to smoke a cigarette when in fact she was the most sophisticated, well-traveled, street-wise, slippery-fingered, nicotine-besotted, sexy Pop-Tart in all New York. (Lose that sexy, he said to himself; Jim's girl, remember, Jim's girl.) Yet she rode the scooter downtown with a bliss-ful, sweet smile, throwing her head back and breath-ing deeply as though she had never before felt such a free and easy breeze upon her face. She peered at the downtown streets curiously, as though she had never seen them; and her shiny blonde hair slipped out from under the helmet and tickled his neck like silk in the wind. And of all the things he had heard about this girl, the only thing that seemed to be true was that she was incredibly pretty.

("Jim's girl," he said to himself as her breasts burned holes in his back. "Jim's Jim's *Jim's* girl.")

At the Dragon Noodle, Dez's neighbor and former friend Choy was waiting with two large takeout orders, already completely congealed in their cardboard cartons. Choy was not angry. He was not hysterical. He refrained from telling Dez all the many historic events that had happened in their neighborhood during the scooter's long absence—how Emily Fu had graduated from Juilliard, signed with the Utah Symphony, and moved to Provo; how Han Tong and Won Tong had met at the Yellow River Saloon and finally settled the Tong wars; how the large moving van across the street had been loaded up with virtually everything Dezmund O'Herlihy owned. No, Choy said nothing of this. What he did say was, "Never again."

"Sorry, man . . ." Dez began.

"Never, ever again," Choy said, getting on the scooter.

"It was an emergency."

"Never, ever, ever, ever . . ."

"We got stuck. . . ."

". . . ever again."

"I'm sorry."

"I understand. Don't ask me again, ever."

Suddenly very tired, Dez climbed the fire escape that led to his loft. Roberta followed in the strange, halting, docile way she had, which was so irreconcilable with what he had heard of Susan.

"People *live* here?" she marveled.

"Yes, people live here!" Dez snapped back. (Offer a homeless woman a couch to sleep on and what does the bitch do? Bitch!)

Down the fire escape came a guy with a box on his shoulder. (Does he say "excuse me"? Does he step aside? No, grumped Dez to himself. I, the boy scout, *I* say "excuse me," *I* step aside.) No sooner did the box carrier pass than another asshole barreled down the stairway with two stereo speakers that looked strangely familiar. On the landing outside his apartment, the whole truth dawned. A third porter appeared with Dez's television set and the vomit-green lamp with the ocher paper shade that Victoria had insisted on bringing with her when she moved in. (An antique, she said. Galveston, circa 1928.)

"Whoa, wait just one minute. What do you think you're doing? Give me that!" Dez said. The moving man did not protest. Dez might be a gentle soul at heart, but once aroused he was clearly not to be messed with. He let the open door of the apartment swing wide. Roberta cowered behind him.

The apartment was stripped naked.

From behind a blue-green plastic partition there came the sound of a man's voice and the elegant laughter of the catastrophic broad Dez had almost succeeded in forgetting during the last several hours.

"That's just great, Victoria," he said. He leaned against the Shaolin Chastity Kung Fu supergraphic that framed his doorway.

"It's my stuff, Dez," Victoria said.

God, she's beautiful, Roberta thought. Look at that gray-and-white duster! Look at that gray broadcloth shirt! Look at that black satin tie! Victoria's dark-red hair was cut short, and her gray eyes were haughty, and she had the carriage of an aristocrat. She might as well be a model in one of those magazines you read only in the beauty parlor. (Just having these thoughts gave Roberta pause. How come Susan knew so much about better women's wear? Was it possible that someone as chic as Susan went to *beauty parlors?*)

"So you just come and take it, right?" Dez said. "No phone call, no discussion, no nothing." He looked with real pity at the pale-haired guy carrying another box for Victoria. "How you doing?" he said. (With a self-restraint that would one day be legend in the motion-picture industry, he did not say, "How you doing, lame-o?")

"Listen, I'm gonna take this stuff down to the Porsche . . ." said Victoria's (now very nervous) new boyfriend.

"I believe some of that is *mine,*" Dez mentioned. "Like the answering machine. And the Charlie Parker record."

"Oh look, you can have it," said Victoria.

"Thank you."

"Why don't I send you a check for the rest?" Victoria looked down on Roberta; she was very tall, this Victoria, almost as tall as Dez. "He's a nice guy," she said. "You'll be happy together." And out she glided, cool and confident as a British official exiting India after the Raj. And the souvenirs she was taking were just as ripped off.

For the first time all day there was a silence. A long, long silence, amplified many times by the emptiness of Dez's apartment.

"Oh, I'm so sorry," Roberta whispered, watching

him walk up and down the bare floors. He looked so gaunt at this moment, even stooped, his veins bulging with anger unexpressed and his strong back sort of hunching. He reminded her of Abe Lincoln. He reminded her of Bjorn Borg in defeat. He reminded her of a miserable widower all alone after the death of his beloved wife. . . . Now where had she read that story?

Roberta tried to think of something to say.

"You know, you could do a lot with this place," she offered. "I mean, there's so much light . . ."

She shut up.

There was really nothing to say.

At the far end of the long apartment, a long table remained. On it there was a kind of machine that Roberta had never seen before. It had spools of film in it, so she assumed it must be for editing. Ceiling-high bookcases on one wall housed dozens of silver film cans, filled, she assumed, with the movies Dez had assembled.

Maybe they were artistic masterpieces.

Maybe they were filthy pornographic sleaze flicks.

Susan wouldn't care one way or the other, but Roberta, who did not know that, felt sure they were artistic masterpieces.

The editing table had no chair anymore. Presumably Victoria had removed it along with everything else. She had left some assorted pillows and blankets, which Dez found in a tumbled mass in the corner, and she had left his clothes.

He crouched down under one of the many large windows in the loft and lit a cigarette. Roberta remained silent because she could see he was trying to keep himself under control.

The pink light of the waning day poured through the window and shined on his light-brown hair. Above him, the top of the Chrysler Building was framed by the window. Across the loft, another bank of windows let in the sunset Day-Glo glitter on the waters of the East River.

A shaggy cat named Cat rubbed up against Roberta, testing her friendliness. She scratched his head and patted his tail. He purred receptively. It was nice to know that Susan enjoyed the company of pets.

Right smack in the middle of the apartment, there was a blue-green partition inlaid with a see-through fish tank. The fish inside caught the sunset light on their silver fins and shimmered pinkly. Roberta smiled. (So Susan also had a thing for fish.)

"What are their names?" she asked.

"The fish? Oh. Clara. Marilyn. Annette. And Doris," Dez answered. "They're all harmless. Not one of them a man-eater."

Roberta felt so bad for him, she wanted to run over to the window and give him a hug. But she didn't dare because her boyfriend, Jim, was Dez's best friend.

"Aw, shit," Dez said softly. "It happens, right?" He plugged in the answering machine he had just barely saved and pressed the message button. On came this voice Roberta had never heard before.

"Oh, uh, hi, Dez, it's, uh, it's Jim here. I'm, uh, just calling to see, you know, if Susan's okay. . . . I'm calling from, uh . . . I don't know where we are . . . some hotel. . . . Where are we, Mitzi? . . . She doesn't know. Look, I'll call you tomorrow, okay? Thanks again for everything. You're a pal, you're a real pal. Bye." Click went the message button.

"That's got to ring some bells," Dez said.

Roberta shook her head.

"Honestly, no," she answered.

He sighed and sagged.

"I need a drink," he said. "You want one?"

"All right. Thank you."

"What'll it be?"

"Oh, whatever you're having. Apple juice, Coke, Perrier . . ."

He glared at her. Really he was up to here with the incredible dingbat persona Jim's girl, Susan, had decided to adopt today!

"Miller or Heineken?"

"All right."

"Which?"

"Oh, uh, either one . . . please."

This Susan sure said please and thank you a lot for a girl with hotel silverware in her suitcase.

Roberta heard Dez groan in the kitchen.

"What's the matter?" she called.

He didn't answer.

Scared to death, she tiptoed into the kitchen. He was leaning against the wall. His dark blue eyes were like stormy oceans. "I don't believe it," he said.

The refrigerator was gone.

■   □   ■

don't believe it," said Susan when she discovered that her Port Authority locker was empty.

This had not yet become the worst week of her life, but it was getting close.

First she discovered that the guy who had shown her such a good time in Atlantic City had been murdered. Then Jimmy had dropped in for an hour, had given her a couple of kisses, and had left town. Then she had tried to swipe a pair of rhinestone boots, but "Tina Turner" had caught her and she had had to part with her pyramid jacket that she loved so much to acquire the boots that she couldn't live without, and she had lost the key to her locker.

Then she had been lured back to the Battery by an ad in The Personals, only to discover that the people who lured her were some blonde witch with red boots and a blond greaseball who looked vaguely familiar.

Then the asshole cab driver who had driven so bumpily that he had made her lipstick smear had insisted that she pay him the full fare, and before she could get the blonde with the red boots to pay, the police had taken her to jail.

So then she had spent six hours in the tank with whores and junkies and husband beaters, and she hadn't dared call Crystal to come down and pay the $9.20 she owed the cab driver because after all, how much can you impose on your friends?

So then she had told the jail matron a story about how she was really the daughter of a major Hollywood agent who threw her out of the house when he caught her in bed with his least-bankable client, and that's why she had no money, and the matron finally had lit her cigarette.

So then she had told the other jail matron how she was really the oldest daughter of an archeology professor who had gotten killed in a cave-in at the pyramids, and now she had to support her sick mother selling buttons on the Battery, and she had spent her last bread on medicine for Mom, so that's why she couldn't pay the cab driver.

The matron, a big, fat Nazi type, had said, "Yeah, yeah."

So Susan had said that all her savings from button selling were locked in a locker at the Port Authority and she didn't have the key, so *now* what was she gonna do?

So the matron had slipped her a crowbar confiscated from some burglar and they had finally released her from jail. So then, feeling better, she had gone to the Port Authority with her crowbar, and wham! All her stuff was gone. Taken undoubtedly by the red-booted witch who had bought her beautiful pyramid jacket and was clearly in cahoots with that blond greaseball.

Where have I seen him? Susan wondered, bopping out onto Eighth Avenue. . . . I've seen him someplace. Did I sleep with him? No, that's impossible, I wouldn't sleep with a guy who has a smile like a limp string bean.

So then it was midnight on Forty-second Street.

A beautiful night—warm, but just a little breezy, with a large, desert moon poised between the twin towers like a gong. The perfume of whistling whores made the streets sweet. The laughter of happy drunks made the streets jingle. Suburban kids, fearing nothing tonight, walked arm in arm from their dockside concerts, singing the Top 40. The gay bars murmured low. Pretty dancers drifted west from a night's work on Broadway, feeling blessed to be living the life they had always wanted.

It was a night to lie on your back and listen to

Jimmy Riddle sing dark blues songs, to think of home, and to tell the truth and cry for love. It was not a night to turn in early and sleep alone.

But Susan had no money: none.

It looked as though she would have to jump the subway turnstile and ride downtown to Crystal's place with every creep and sociopath in New York. Worst of all, the Port Authority ladies' room mirror told her she was getting a *zit*.

Susan looked closely at herself in the mirror. She adjusted her bellyless black lace blouse and her big black Jewish star. She redid her eyes and her mouth. Who could she find in this neighborhood at this hour of the night who would help her get home without her having to defend herself with the crowbar? Someone respectable, someone cute but nonviolent.

She decided to pick up an actor.

She found him browsing in an all-night bookstore near Manhattan Plaza, lingering at the map section, and on his exceedingly high cheekbones he had a look of longing.

"Thinking of going to Kyoto?" she asked.

"Thinking of going anywhere but another audition."

"Let's go to Egypt."

"I haven't got enough money for the fare."

"You got enough money for the map?"

"Not that either."

Shit, she thought. An *out-of-work* actor! They always broke her heart!

She stole a map of Japan for him and a map of Egypt for herself, and he took her to the West Bank

Café. All he could afford was coffee. Luckily, they met a Broadway dancer who had the hots for him. She took one look at Susan and began to cry.

"Come pee with me," said Susan in the spirit of sisterhood. When they were alone in the ladies' room, she made the dancer an offer. "Give me cab fare home plus $10, and I promise I'll never go near him again. Cross my heart."

"Done," said the lovesick girl, shaking Susan's hand.

As Susan slipped out the back door through the kitchen (swiping half a head of lettuce on the way), she noticed that her new friends were already making out at the bar. She hoped they would both be famous one day.

That night, Susan slept alone on the green sofa in Crystal's canary-yellow apartment. She started to dream and got nervous and woke herself up. Crystal wasn't home from the Magic Club yet. Susan fell asleep again and dreamed of Jim.

He was lying in a huge, messy bed, running a dangerously high fever. His large, soft eyes were rolling upward in his head; only the whites showed. He tossed and moaned. Pain covered him in a cold sweat.

"Susan . . ." he sang in his delirium "Susan, baby, don't let me go. . . . Don't let me die alone in Buffa- loooo. . . ."

His silly lyrics tripped her; she laughed and fell laughing into the bed with him. He grabbed her. He rolled her into the clammy white sheets. He stopped her breath with his cold, white teeth. His pale arms locked around her neck, choking her, killing her. . . .

"This is what it means to love," he sang. "This is how it feels to need. . . ."

Susan woke up screaming.

■   □   ■

Across the river in Fort Lee, Gary Glass called the police.

"I don't know where my wife is," he said. "She hasn't come home. It's not like her."

The policeman on the other end of the line laughed, but Gary persevered.

"My shy, repressed little wife has never done anything like this, ever," he said. "I'm glad you think this is funny, officer, but you know what I think? I think she's in trouble. Maybe she's had an accident. Maybe somebody mugged her in New York. Yes, that's what must have happened. She went to New York to pick up the car radio she forgot to pick up the other day, and the minute she finished getting it installed, somebody mugged her and stole it. Doesn't that happen all the time? I mean, car radios getting stolen. . . . This was an extraspecial terrific stereo; it had eight speakers. . . ."

"Has she got another guy on the side, Mr. Glass?"

"I'm telling you, she's been mugged!"

"Is anything missing from your house? Look around."

"I'm telling you, she's had an accident!"

"Housewives from Fort Lee do this all the time, Mr. Glass."

"Please, officer, you don't know my wife."

"Do *you*?"

Gary lost his temper.

"Who appointed you Dr. Ruth?" Gary hollered. "Would you please stop psychoanalyzing my situation here and start looking for Roberta?"

"Okay, okay," said the cop, "don't get defensive. What's she wearing?"

"She must be wearing the new jacket she bought; it's not around anywhere. You can't miss that jacket."

Gary described the pyramid jacket.

"Please describe her car, Mr. Glass."

"Right, the car. You can't miss the car. It's a brand-new black Ford convertible. The license plate says 'TUB N SPA.' "

"What?"

Gary spelled it for him.

"You got a picture? Find a picture of your wife, and we'll be over in a little while to get it."

"How long is 'a little while'?"

The cop hung up.

Gary looked on the refrigerator, but all the pictures hanging there were pictures of him. He looked through a photo album, but all the pictures in it were pictures of him and his in-laws and Roberta's beloved dead dog Dorothy. Finally he dug in the dining-room sideboard and found Roberta's wedding picture.

She was really cute as a bride, with her arms full of white lilies and her fluffy veil and her big, hopeful grin. Gary remembered how nervous he was on their wedding night, because it had been so many years since he had made love to a near-virgin. He remembered how nervous Roberta's liberated mother had made him, arriving at the wedding in a Land-Rover with a boyfriend half her age. ("Take care, Gary," said his late father. "Sometimes the tendency to split is genetic among women, just like big tits.")

I'm a little nervous about all this, he wanted to say to the impassive cops when they arrived. I'm used to coming home from my evening meetings and finding Roberta cuddled up in our bed, watching romantic old movies. She wears white pajamas mostly; she's a wonderful cook.

When the police left, Gary called his friend Larry Stillman, the dentist. But Larry wasn't home.

"If your tooth is killing you and you haven't got any Percodan," Dr. Stillman's machine said, "drink yourself into a stupor and I'll call you back in the morning."

■   □   ■

Leslie Glass watched her brother, Gary, as he rummaged voraciously through her refrigerator.

"Face the truth," she said. "Roberta has left you."

"Roberta couldn't have left me. That's impossible! She's got everything a woman could want. She's got everything!"

"Did you tell the police about the jacket?" Leslie snapped.

"Yes," he answered, pulling out the grapes, the Muenster cheese, the tomatoes, the pickles, the seeded rye.

"Did you tell them she left her wedding ring in the soap dish?"

"Where's the mayonnaise?"

"You didn't tell them, did you?" Leslie snarled. "You were embarrassed to tell them she took off her wedding ring before she left you!"

"I *told* them she wasn't wearing a wedding ring, Les. Will you lay off?"

Leslie Glass swished back and forth across her kitchen, sweeping the floor with her azure peignoir, fidgety as Queen Isabella waiting for word from the *Santa Maria.* She drummed her fingernails on the kitchen counter. She gnashed her teeth. She looked down at her older brother as he constructed his gross sandwich, and she noticed with some delight that he was starting to lose his hair.

"The police seem to think Roberta's having an affair," he said.

"Oh my God!" cried Leslie. "Maybe she is!"

"That's ridiculous," he said casually. "Roberta is not having an affair. She's much too uptight." Now he was crouching in front of the refrigerator, squinting like a ravenous lion who must make his selection from a herd of zebra.

"That is a perfectly horrible thing to say!" Leslie hissed. (Swish, drum, gnash.)

"Don't you have any lettuce?"

"Of course I have lettuce!" (Gnash, double gnash.) "It's in the crisper. That's where lettuce is supposed to be!"

"What's the 'crisper'?"

Leslie called upon her small reserve of pity. "God, Gary," she said, "you are such a *prince!* What are you going to do now that Roberta has left you? You'll starve."

"Roberta has not left me, Leslie. Where the hell is the mayonnaise? This refrigerator is so damn full a person can't find anything in it!"

"Don't worry, big brother, soon your refrigerator will be so empty you will be able to see your reflection in its rear wall." Leslie slammed the mayonnaise down on the table and drummed her nails on the lid. *She* knew why Roberta had left Gary. "I suppose you're proud of the way you've been running around with Becky Shuman."

"Becky and I are not running around!" Gary protested. "We are having a perfectly respectable affair!" He ate half the cheese, then he put the other half on his sandwich. It was getting to be a very big sandwich. "I didn't know you knew about Becky...."

"When will you learn that I know about everything!" roared Leslie. "I knew the first time you made it with Consuela in the laundry room, and I knew the first time Daddy made it with Consuela, too!"

Gary gagged on his sandwich. "Daddy made it with Consuela?"

"I knew that you ran over Harriet Levine's pet snake the first day you got your driver's license and you buried him in the backyard under the mock orange!"

"Enough, Leslie."

"And everybody thought he just slithered away! *Ha!*"

"Did Daddy make it with Consuela before me or after me or during me?"

Leslie suddenly gave up swishing and drumming and gnashing and took up leaning. She leaned over

Gary, narrow eyed, all knowing, oppressive as a pillar of the synagogue.

"Gareeeee, let me ask you something. . . ."

"What?"

"Does Roberta have . . . orgasms?"

"Orgasms?"

"You have heard of them, haven't you?"

"I need a drink, Les. Apple juice, Coke, Perrier, whatever you've got. . . ."

"I mean, maybe the reason she left you was because you weren't satisfying her."

"Leslie! Not everybody is obsessed with orgasms! Some people just . . . have them."

"Did *she*?"

"Okay, what's the story? Did Phil Donahue do a show on orgasms or something?"

"You really are a *pig*, you know? You are disgusting! You are just like Daddy! At least I understand about *feelings!*"

Gary got his own apple juice. "I feel," he said. "I feel."

"No wonder Roberta left you."

"Will you stop saying that!"

Larry Stillman stumbled sleepily in from the bedroom, his longish, curly black hair all disheveled.

"Larry?" said Gary.

"Hi, Gary," Larry said. "Any word from Roberta?"

Gary Glass smiled nastily at his sister. "Fast work, Les," he said. (So *that's* why she was wearing the azure peignoir! Pillar of the synagogue, my ass!)

"What're we eating?" Larry Stillman asked. "Oh, look at that chicken. That looks great. Let's eat the chicken."

"Please, Larry," Leslie pleaded, "the chicken's for tomorrow." Larry and Gary ate the chicken anyway. "I can't believe the two of you are *eating* in the middle of a crisis!"

"We're nervous," Gary said, working on a wing.

"Then take a Valium like a normal person!" screamed Leslie. Out she stormed, at her wit's end in a blither of azure acetate, swishing and drumming and gnashing.

"She's got great teeth," Larry Stillman commented to his future brother-in-law.

■　□　■

While her wedding portrait was slowly working its way through the NYPD bureaucracy toward Missing Persons, Roberta Glass was drinking gin on a rooftop in Chinatown.

A glowing skylight lit the roof. Cat rubbed his loins against it voluptuously, purring to the glow. Roberta rubbed her face against the moon.

Dezmund O'Herlihy sat near her, eating Chinese food from a carton with chopsticks. He had made friends with Choy again; few people could hold a grudge against Dez for long. Because the skylight bred shadows and the breeze blew her hair across her face, Roberta knew she was half hidden from Dez and could look at him freely and he wouldn't see the magic little fire in her eyes.

Roberta marveled at how brilliantly Dez had relaxed since the crisis with Victoria at sunset. He wasn't worried anymore at all. Clearly he was a Type

B personality (now where had Susan read about that?) who could lose his tensions in the pleasures of the moment—the pleasure of this breeze, this carton of har shew ding, this quiet, carefree hour with Jim's girl, Susan. A guy in a blue window played the saxophone. . . . Roberta couldn't tell where the window was in the landscape of rooftops. It seemed to float among the moonlit clouds. . . . She had seen something, heard something like this, in a painting once, or in a show, or in another country long ago. . . .

"Jim said a friend of yours got killed outside your hotel in Atlantic City," Dez said. "He was pretty worried. That's why he asked me to show up in Battery Park."

Roberta was stunned. She took a long drink of gin. What kind of a life had she been leading?

"Killed *dead?*" Roberta marveled.

"Sorta goes with the territory, doesn't it, Susan?"

She searched and searched her empty memory. How could anybody forget a murder?

"Maybe I know who did it," she said, appalling herself. "Oh, I wish I could remember."

Dez crossed his long legs. His knee grazed her foot; he pulled it away quickly, so she wouldn't get the wrong idea. But he didn't know she already had the wrong idea because he couldn't see the magic little fire in her eyes, couldn't feel her wondering what his legs smelled like, whether his knees were soft.

"Maybe you were the killer," he suggested.

"Oh, no," she said emphatically. Susan wouldn't kill anyone! Or would she? Oh my God . . . "I should probably lay low for a while, huh?"

"It might be a wise idea," Dez suggested. He

chuckled and scissored some more rice into his mouth. Obviously he didn't really think she was a killer; else why would he sit here on this rooftop so comfortable with her, so quiet and easy and comfortable?

Roberta was beginning to feel a little bothered by the deep shadows. Maybe she *wanted* him to see her eyes better. She wanted to touch his mouth and run the shaggy hair of his eyebrows between her fingers.

She took another long drink of gin. It burned her inside, but it did change her mind.

"So you don't know who the guy on the dock was?" Dez was saying. "The blond guy . . . he had his hands in your . . . I know it sounds crazy, but he looked like he was feeling your ears."

"I don't remember," she answered. She felt her ears, her little earrings so unlike those others in her suitcase. Her ears were hot.

"Maybe a jilted lover?" Dez suggested.

"Oh, I don't think so," Roberta said. Where had she heard that before? "I don't think so, no, I don't. . . ." Maybe this man whom Dez spoke of had really been her lover. Maybe Susan had a thousand lovers, maybe she was the queen of the night and pounded the flesh of men and made off with their hearts. "Maybe he was," she said. "Maybe he was my lover and I left him for Jim."

Dez fell silent. He took a drink from the bottle. On the rim of his jaw a little nerve shivered. Roberta wondered if he had hair on his belly.

"You know something?" said Dez. "You are not at all what I expected."

"You're not what I expected either," said Roberta.

Why did she say that? How could a woman who remembers nothing expect *anything* different from what she was getting? The saxophone had begun striking the same chords in Roberta's body that the little blue motor scooter had discovered, and that made her nervous. Calm down, she told herself. You are Susan. You are *Susan!* A woman like Susan would *expect* the night to be perfect, she would expect the moon to be magic, and she would fully expect the man to be an angel, chuckling, sort of thin, with large, strong hands so clearly gentle and skilled that you wanted to put them inside your shirt for safekeeping. . . . Roberta sat on her legs.

"How did you meet Jim?" she asked Dez. "Did you grow up together?"

"No, we met in an editing room. I was directing a video for Dry Bones. . . ."

"Who?"

"Jim's group. He's a musician. I was directing a video for the group and we didn't have much money and the song was about passion but the girls we had were cold, so I had to put in the heat in the edit. Jim came into the editing room and sat behind me at the console. He didn't tell me what to do; he just watched; he likes learning things. I asked him to sing. I was trying to make the still, cold girls move, and I needed the beat . . . so he sang . . . 'This is what it means to love . . . this is how it feels to . . . need. . . .'" Dez stopped talking. He turned his face away. But it was too late. Jim's girl, Susan, had stopped sitting on her legs.

"Is he tall?" Roberta asked, smiling a little. "I mean Jim."

"He's about medium."

She leaned toward him very slightly.

"Is he sort of thin?" she asked.

Dez took another drink from the bottle. "Sort of . . . sort of, uh . . . my build." He glanced at her; she was coming closer; he noticed this little fire. . . .

"What color eyes does he have?" asked the queen of the night. Her hair glowed. Her skin glowed. Dez knew she was going to kiss him the way you know there's going to be fireworks over New York Harbor on the Fourth, and he could not keep from grinning.

"Blue," he said.

She kissed him and the glow filled his mouth.

"I'm sorry," she cried, pulling herself out of his arms. "I'm sorry!" Dez hid his face in his hands, and his hands shook. "I don't know what happened," she said. "I just . . ." She laughed self-consciously. "Oh, I'm sorry."

The breeze died. The moon hid. The rain began to fall.

■   □   ■

I t fell like bongo pops at first, in big drops, few and far between, and then more insistently, and then in lightning-whitened sheets that shook buildings and even shook the steel nerves of the New Yorkers. Explosions of thunder kept them sleepless. Finales of thunder reminded them of their worst, their very worst fears.

Susan tiptoed past her friend Crystal who was softly snoring and stood naked in front of the open refrigerator, cooling her heavenly body, trying to get over her dream. Maybe an apple would distract her —but there were none. Maybe a beer—but there was only one, and that flat. Who the hell was the blond man with the black clothes? Why did the recollection of him make her skin crawl with anxiety? She had no enemies, no one to be afraid of, and yet she trembled thinking of that light, almost-white hair. Maybe it was her dream . . . the white sheets in the dream . . . white sheets wrapped like swaddling on a mummy. . . . The last time she had seen Bruce Meeker, he was wrapped in the sheets of their bed . . . and he was alive. . . .

■   □   ■

Gary Glass did not go to bed.
He kept himself awake by watching old movies in the kitchen, as his wife, Roberta, used to do.
Finally the phone rang.
Gary tried not to stop breathing. He assumed it was the police. He assumed they would have news ranging from "Nothing yet" to "She's got a flat on the Turnpike" to "She's dead."
But he was wrong.
It was not the police.
It was Leslie, his sister.
"When you were a little boy," she said, "you were always scared of thunder. So I just called to tell you not to be scared. Roberta's probably got a flat on the Turnpike, and in such a big storm she can't get to a phone, and I don't want you to be scared; it's only thunder."

■ □ ■

Wayne Nolan thanked the thunder and the lightning for keeping him awake. He was sitting in the nondescript black car, under the Dragon Noodle sign. He ran the windshield wipers so he wouldn't miss Dez and Roberta if they left the apartment. He couldn't fall asleep. He couldn't. He couldn't. He didn't dare fall asleep. . . .

■ □ ■

Susan remembered where she had seen him.
  It was in a snapshot in Bruce Meeker's wallet.
  "Who's the greaseball?" she had asked.
"My ex-partner," Bruce had said. "Let's hope we don't run into him on the boardwalk. It could ruin our vacation."

■ □ ■

Only Dez and Roberta slept well and long and late, separated on opposite sides of the iridescent fish tank.
  Dez tossed awhile before he fell asleep. He wished Victoria hadn't taken away the bed so he would not have to sleep in the sleeping bag on the floor (Roberta had the mattress). He wished Victoria were still coiled in his arms so he would not have to deal with the disturbing presence of Jim's girl, Susan. He wished Susan would stop having

her guilt trip and come over on his side of the fish tank.

He wished he didn't wish that.

Before she fell asleep, Roberta laughed at the storm outside, thinking how terrific it was to be Susan.

Chapter 4

Early Friday morning, after the storm, Gilda the bartender decided to clean the Magic Club.

"Enough with the junk!" she declared. "One sentimental woman and a bunch of dummies cannot single-handedly preserve the history of the living stage! Get rid of the sets, clear out the costumes, call the Smithsonian!"

Gilda's son, Ray, called the Smithsonian, but they said their theatrical triviabilia collection was full up. He called the Museum of the City of New York, but they said they were interested only in things Dutch. ASCAP sent a lawyer to look through the dozen or so cartons of sheet music left over from old strip-show auditions; however, she found nothing that might be useful in an out-of-court settlement.

Gilda felt certain someone would want the larger-than-life-size papier-mâché head of Joe Louis disguised as a Confucian schoolmaster. Nobody did.

Nobody: not even the Schomberg. The great head stayed on its high shelf in the ladies' dressing room, housing mice.

Gilda had better luck with the Dramatists Guild. They took Siamese-twin end tables which, Gilda said, had originated with the original *King and I*. They also took half a dozen miniature gravestones that had once been used in a puppet version of *Our Town,* feeling these would make terrific bookends.

However, even the guild wasn't desperate enough to accept the Sick Ibsenite Sofa.

This sofa—"a neorococo Victorian Scandinavian one-of-a-kind," Gilda said—was covered with soot-green velveteen upholstery. Two of its legs had rotted and fallen off. Its underbelly dangled down intestinally, in sickening yellow globs. It had been slashed repeatedly with knives.

"But why, Gilda?" Crystal would ask. "Why would anybody slash a one-of-a-kind sofa?"

Gilda answered that it is not an easy thing for an actor to communicate that he has inherited venereal disease and his brain is disintegrating and he is going mad when Ibsen has not given him any lines to that effect; therefore, actors sometimes resorted to sofa slashing to make their point.

Gilda finally gave up on giving away the sofa. She asked Ray the manager, and Ian the magician to carry it out to the street. "Eventually it'll biodegrade," she said confidently.

Ray and Ian placed the sofa adjacent to the Magic Club's bullet-riddled front door, on the opposite side from the derelict, while back inside Gilda began mopping the history of the living stage off the Magic

Club's floors, singing all the while a classic ditty called "Come on Home to the Kennel, Calvin, Your Bitch Is Hot Tonight," originally performed (Gilda said) by the incomparable Velva Spangles in "More T and A of 1912."

Crystal came in for her 9:00 A.M. rehearsal, the sleep still crumbly in her eyes. Gilda left off mopping and gave her a cup of coffee. The bright sunshine streamed in through the bullet holes in the front door.

"Tell me about the bullet holes, Gilda, please," said Crystal.

"No, my child, I cannot. Now drink your juice and eat your Twinkie."

"Please, Gilda," Crystal pleaded. "I love gossip. I love stories. Please tell me. I promise I won't say a word to Susan." And because she had been living with Susan for twenty-four hours she added, "Cross my heart."

Gilda remained adamant.

"Some things are better off buried and left to crystallize like the great sequoia," she said sadly. She patted Crystal's hand and cleaned up her Twinkie crumbs.

If Crystal had been smarter, she would have asked Kaminsky the dummy, who knew the whole story of the bullet holes, unfortunately from firsthand experience.

Right now, Kaminsky was lounging on the soot-green sofa, lifting his face to the morning sun, trying to catch a few more freckles to make his act more appealing. His friend the derelict sprawled on the pavement, engrossed in a fresh copy of the *New York Morning Downer* which had been bought by a passerby but immediately dropped because it was just too depressing to read on such a lovely morning.

The pigeons basked, fluffing their feathers. Big, bright reflecting puddles had collected in the potholes during last night's torrential rain. Wonder Woman and Claudette Colbert, feeling young and gay again, splashed in them and sang Ira Gershwin songs.

"Ah, how these deathless melodies warm the cockles of an old dummy's heart," sighed Kaminsky contentedly. "But what do young people like Dez and Roberta and Jim and Susan know of music such as this? I hear tell their audio nerves have all been damaged by amplification; they can't even *hear* good, much less do they care for the theme music of our lives and times. The Great War, the Great Depression, all our 'Rhapsodies in Blue' are but ancient dramas to these young folk, vague and melodramatic as Ibsen's plays. Do they study the lessons of history? No, no, a thousand times no. All they wanna do is make a living and get laid."

Claudette stopped singing Gershwin.

"But, Kaminsky," she said, "isn't that exactly the same thing *we* wanted to do?"

"Speak for yourself, ditzface!" roared Wonder Woman.

Gilda came out with her vacuum cleaner and vacuumed the whole group. "Watch out for my toupee!" Kaminsky warned. Then Gilda carried Wonder Woman and Claudette Colbert back inside and draped capes over them once again, tiptoeing so as not to disturb the rehearsal.

Ian and Crystal were practicing a new trick.

Ian was going to put Crystal in a box and saw her

in half. All she had to do was scrunch up her legs into her end of the box and press the button that wiggled her fake feet on the other end of the box.

Crystal scrunched up fine. But she couldn't see the foot-wiggling button. She had to grope for it, and so the trick lost its timing. The rehearsal was not going well.

Ian leaned down over Crystal as she scrunched, immobile and helpless in the box. He was wearing his baby-blue leisure suit and his white bucks, the outfit Crystal most hated.

"How about a hand job under the pinball machine?" Ian asked.

"Get me out of this box, you turd," Crystal said.

"Five minutes in the kitchen," Ian suggested, wagging his orange eyebrows.

"I can't feel my legs, Ian!"

"You don't realize how beautiful you are without your glasses, Crystal. I've had the hots for you for a whole year. Don't deny me any longer. Ten minutes, fifteen minutes tops, that's all it'll take a smart girl like you to blow my head off, and if you do, I promise I'll let you wear your glasses in the act."

Crystal could not see, but she could *hear*, Ian unzipping the pants of his baby-blue leisure suit.

"*Gilda!*" she screamed. "*Ray! Gilda! Helpppppp!*"

"You're fired," Ian said, zipping up his pants.

"Oh no, you don't, Ian. . . ."

Ian opened the box, and Crystal unwound like a python.

". . . You don't get to fire me because *I quit!*"

Gilda came running in from the bar. Ray came running in from the kitchen.

"Crystal, Crystal, don't quit. Ian's a wonderful person. He's a devoted husband and father," Ray protested.

"Give me my glasses!" Crystal screamed. "Where are my glasses? Give me my glasses so I can kick this prick's dick into his white bucks!"

"Get her away from me!" Ian yelled. "Not only is she blind, she also talks dirty! I don't want her in my act another minute!"

"Ian, Ian, don't get crazy," Gilda said. "Crystal is a good woman. I'm sure you guys can work this out."

Crystal retrieved her glasses and aimed a deadly kick at Ian, but Ian grabbed Kaminsky the dummy just in time and shielded himself. Thus, it was Kaminsky who took the full force of the terrible blow.

"It's lucky I have no feeling below the waist," he commented.

"May you all be pecked to death by pigeons!" Crystal screamed, her last line at the Magic Club.

Susan was waiting for her outside. She was sitting on the Sick Ibsenite Sofa in the sun.

To cheer herself up after her icky dream of the night before, Susan had decided to wear red. She had swiped a red T-shirt from a construction site and wrapped Crystal's torn red tights around her hair, and on her full lips she had her most dashing vermilion splash. She was entertaining herself by watching the underparts of a workman standing above her on a ladder, who was polishing the *M* and the *G* and the *C* on the "Magic Club" sign as part of Gilda's clean-sweep program.

Crystal almost walked right under the ladder.

"Stop!" yelled Susan, the human red light. "Not under the ladder!" Crystal walked around the ladder and plumped down on the sofa next to Susan.

"That miserable scumbag!" she grumped. " Maybe I should have slept with him. . . ."

"He fired you?" Susan said.

Crystal nodded.

"Man," Susan said, patting her friend, "some witch steals my clothes, Meeker gets pushed out a hotel window, and now you get fired."

"No offense," Crystal commented, "but bad luck really seems to be following you around."

Susan gazed up with regret at the workman. She really had been looking forward to meeting with him when he descended. But Crystal needed her, that was clear. "Look, we're both free now," Susan said. "Let's just go to the movies. *Underwater Werewolf* and *Blob of the Slime Bog* are playing at the Bleecker Street Cinema. Come on."

She pulled Crystal to her feet, grinning. Crystal caught her light and brightened.

"I'll pay for the movie if you pay for the popcorn," Crystal said, as they walked off arm in arm.

Susan grabbed her playfully by the ass, and she jumped and giggled. "How much is popcorn?" Susan asked.

■　□　■

Cat announced the break of morning to Dez by jumping on him.

Dez did not stir from his sleeping bag. Cat sat on his naked shoulders, careful not to scratch him, and watched the pretty little fish—Clara and Marilyn, Annette and Doris—swim in their fish tank. "Look, but don't touch" was their motto. Cat licked his chops.

Through the glass greenly, Cat could see the new mistress of this household cuddled in her makeshift bed. He considered insinuating himself among her pillows and quilts; she looked so nice and soft and warm. But then he decided to keep watch over the fish tank, because eventually—if not today, then tomorrow; if not this year, then next—the tank would develop a crack, then a leak, then a seismic split, and the four pretty little fish would come tumbling down in a cascade of water to satisfy Cat's hunger. Until that day, Cat was waiting. Patiently. Licking his chops.

Dez woke up thinking he was underwater.

Why is that? he asked himself.

Oh yeah, probably because the feature he was projecting this weekend was *Underwater Werewolf*.

When he sat up, he saw the fish. Those are your own beloved fish, he told himself; you are not underwater.

Then he saw the mermaid.

Roberta Glass, whom Dez O'Herlihy knew as Susan, was visible through the fish tank. She was naked from the waist up, pulling on a black-and-green sequin-spangled dress that glittered like fish scales. She was as untouchable to Dez as the fish to Cat, but he took an extra thirty seconds to realize that this was not a dream and that she didn't know he was looking at her, and then he took another thirty seconds just to look at her freely, enjoying the extraordinary pleasure of the moment. When he felt himself starting to get hard again, he dropped down into his sleeping bag, grabbing Cat and pretending to be asleep.

For Dez O'Herlihy, the whole experience with this Susan felt complicated only because of the offscreen presence of Jimmy Riddle. In the several years they had known each other, Dez and Jimmy had come to depend on each other for an awful lot. They were of a peculiar generation of American men who had been too young to fight but not too young to lose— Dez, in fact, had lost his older brother—and neither took life's rewards lightly or expected to find friendship every day just lying around.

Dez respected Jimmy. He knew Jimmy was honest, and he felt that Jimmy was talented, really talented— not like most of these bellowing assholes who called themselves musicians, but a real singer, the kind who could sing you a song you had never heard before so profoundly you would know the words forever after.

Dez himself loved music, jazz as much as rock, and regretted that he had not continued taking piano when his mother gave him the chance. He couldn't sing either, but he listened well, and he knew that Jimmy would be famous one day because he knew that good sound rises.

One night during the rock-video shoot that had brought them together, Jimmy and Dry Bones fell afoul of some chain-swinging teenagers in a Pittsburgh nightclub. It wasn't just high spirits; it was angel dust. The customers took off. The management called the cops. The band fought back.

High up in the fly space, Dez secured the camera and left it running. Then he calmly leaped into the tangle of bodies and chains and chairs and over-turned tables and crawled through the broken glass out the back door to his van. He calmly drove the van through the front window of the club, picked up Jimmy, the band, and the camera and sped away.

After that, the cops arrived.

The freaked-out teenage chain gang said in court that Dry Bones had started the fight, but nobody believed them because Dez had the whole episode on tape.

"You are one cool customer," Jimmy said to Dez. "Remind me to buy you a beer when I get this damn cast off."

In the winter, Dez finished his first short film. It was about his sister-in-law, Meg, and her son, Sam.

Meg had been nineteen when she had become a widow ten years ago, and she had never remarried. She took the viewer on a tour through her apartment in Queens and the shoe store where she worked as a saleslady. She tried to describe her husband, Dez's brother, but really she had only known him for a year before he left for Vietnam, and as she talked she realized she had not known this fallen boy very much at all, and was beginning to forget him. And the more she forgot her dead husband, the more invisible she felt herself. Her life and times were being forgotten even as they happened, and she could not make her son understand unless she asked him to live in the past. And she didn't think she ought to do that. The resulting silence in her house rode her, crushed her, erased her.

Well, people cried when they saw Dez's short movie about Meg. Because nobody wants to be invisible.

And everybody understands how close they are to that.

So the movie got chosen to be in a little summer film festival downtown at the Public Theater. The festival was called "Independent Shorts." Dez's mother and father came from Staten Island to see the movie; Meg and her mother and father and Sam came, too; also Meg's new boyfriend. A girl named Victoria stood, tall and classy, at the end of the lobby, surrounded by men, sipping champagne, and leveling her gray eyes at Dez.

Dry Bones was performing in Arizona, so Jim could not attend.

The audience settled. The lights went down. The critics poised their ballpoints. The movie began. Dez stood in the back of the theater, feeling—just the way old Henrik Ibsen had—that somebody would soon stand up and scream: "Where's the talentless fool who created this abomination? Let's kill him!"

A latecomer ran in, looking for an aisle seat, all out of breath. It was dark, but even in the dark, Dez knew it was Jimmy. "I'm sorry I'm late, man," he whispered. "The plane was flying around in circles for an hour."

The audience cried.

The movie won first prize. The critics called Dez a filmmaker to be watched.

But for Dez, the evening's big gift was that he had a buddy who would run off a stage in Phoenix, leave his band and his brothers and their wives, and fly for five hours to New York just to be there . . . just to be there.

It was very hard to screw over such a friend, no

matter what great tits this girl Susan had. Although, Dez felt bound to admit, she certainly was a big departure for Jim, who usually preferred tough, aggressive women, Executive Mogul types, magazine editors, successful trial lawyers, very often smarter and older and richer and taller than Jimmy himself.

Dez had never wanted one of Jimmy's women before. Jimmy's women unnerved him, the way they grabbed the check and understood the wines and never needed help.

Dez was a sucker for women who needed help.

He had perfected a technique with the new breed of technically industrious female who did carpentry and carried gigantic beams and panes of glass, typified by the girl grips who were showing up on movie sets with tools clanking on their asses. With unerring sensitivity, Dez allowed these women to prove themselves beyond doubt. Then, when they had made whatever point they needed to make and could accept his assistance without any political backlash, he moved in with a helping hand, and, invariably, scored.

Thus it had been with Victoria.

She had first engrossed him by bobbling a tray of champagne glasses at the party after "Independent Shorts." She said she was working for the Arts Council but really she was a sculptor. She welded and hammered and smelted semiprecious metal totems, she said, but actually understood nothing of serving champagne.

"Well, that's okay," Dez said in his soft, rather nasal voice. "Even brilliant women can't be expected to know everything."

Victoria fell into his bed like a leaf off a tree, just that easy.

But this Susan was different.

She was not one of Dez's postfeminist pushovers.

She was not one of Jimmy's high-flying power lovers.

She was . . . herself. Part little girl, wishing; part queen of the night, groping. Dez had never met anyone like her.

He could hear her approach, jingling. She scratched Cat's head and touched Dez's shoulder. Since he had been pretending to sleep, he now pretended to wake up.

"Hmmm?"

"Dez? Dez? Want to go out to breakfast with me?"

Jim's girl, Susan, was standing above him wearing the green sequined dress and the pyramid jacket and yards of chains and pearls and torn black stockings and lots of makeup.

"What have you got on?" Dez asked. "Some sort of disguise?"

"You don't like it?"

"No, it's, uh, it's . . . " Dez tried not to laugh; after all . . . "It's sort of charming."

She grinned and stretched a crisp $100 bill above his head.

"My treat," she said.

"What'd you do, rob a bank?"

"I don't know. Maybe." She laughed mischievously. Obviously, this bout of amnesia was beginning to be fun for her. She produced a book of matches. "I thought we could go to this place," she said, "because I found these matches in my case and maybe it's a place I hang out with Jim and people will know me there." Dez scrutinized the matches. Gunny's, over on Centre Street. "I'll go out on the landing and wait for you to get dressed," she said.

Dez couldn't believe her! She was decked out like a whore and she had the manners of his mother!

He decided that, if he was going to go out to breakfast with her, he would wear a disguise, too—so he put on his plaid jacket and his black shirt and his little short-brimmed hat, which made him look a bit tough (like *Rocky I*, Dez thought, while he was still collecting for the mob).

After all, you never knew what you might get into with Susan.

She could conceivably meet another jilted lover, one who would *not* shuffle and stagger away agreeably like the blond guy, so it couldn't hurt to look tough. On the other hand, Susan might get some more of her terrific ideas and pull him into an alley and attempt rape, so it couldn't hurt to wear some of that good-smelling aftershave his folks had given him for his twenty-eighth birthday. On the other hand, she might just order his breakfast and then refuse to pay—he had heard she did that—so it couldn't hurt to pack $20.

They walked over to Gunny's on the sunny sides of all the streets. People stared at her. She seemed to enjoy that.

They couldn't get a table in the crowded luncheonette. So they sat at the counter.

"So, what do you think?" Dez asked. "Anyone look familiar?"

There were reporters from the New York *Mirror*,

which had its offices around the corner; a couple of cops drinking coffee on the cuff; assorted old ladies chatting; there were some construction workers, a model or two, salesmen checking their morning appointments, nobody Jim's girl, Susan, recognized.

"I found this postcard in the case," she said. (It was the Magic Club card that Crystal had desperately sent to Susan in Chicago.) "I thought I'd go there this afternoon."

Dez had never been to the Magic Club. He didn't really believe in magic.

"Do you know what you're having?" he asked.

"What are you having?"

"Well, it's your treat, right?"

"Yeah, I got money."

"So I'll have blueberry blintzes."

"Oooh, that sounds good," she said, "I'll have that, too."

Dez hailed the waitress. She was serving a new customer, completely hidden behind an E-Man comic. "When you get a chance . . ." Dez said politely.

"You can stay," said the waitress. "But she's gotta go."

"What?" Dez said.

"Nick!" yelled the waitress. "It's that crazy girl with the jacket!"

"What?" said Jim's girl, Susan.

Nick, the manager of Gunny's, came out from behind the cash register and hauled Susan by the armpits off her counter stool and started shoving her out the door.

"What's going on?" Susan cried. "You know me?"

"Yeah, I know you want a free meal," Nick said. "Go someplace else."

"I've got money!" she yelled. "I can pay!"

"I don't want your money. I want you out of here."

"Hey, whoa, wait just one minute here. Stop pushing her around!" Dez protested.

"Mind your own business!" Nick said.

"This *is* my business!"

"So, good. So you go too, out, *out*, both of you! You're lucky I don't press charges!" Nick was about a foot taller than Dez. He threw Dez out the door on his ass. The hat fell off. So much for looking tough.

Dez sat calmly on the pavement. "Rule number one," he said, "was no drama."

"Yes, I know. I'm so sorry!" Susan cried.

He allowed her to help him up. "I don't think I want to spend any more time with you, Susan. I mean, a guy could blow his whole week trying to avoid the people you seem to have offended."

"I'm sorry," she said. "I'm so sorry."

"I'm going to work."

"Please forgive me, Dez. Don't be mad. . . ."

"Why don't I drop you off at the Magic Club and later on you can come back home and get your stuff and we'll just call it quits, okay?"

"Are you sure you're not angry?"

"I don't get angry. I stay calm, that's what I do."

They climbed into a taxi.

"Please don't be angry. You're not still angry, are you?"

"Forget it," Dez said. "Here's where you get off."

"You're a real pal, Dez," she said. "I'll tell Jim." She pressed his hand, and he watched her jingle off into the Magic Club, which smelled of Top Job.

Oh, I am a real pal, Dez thought. She'll tell Jim what a pal I am. Shit. I didn't need this aggravation. I'm going to go to work and stay out of trouble and concentrate on the classic green filter techniques of ersatz underwater cinematography.

Back at Gunny's, Nick the proprietor and Aida the waitress were telling the cops that, last year, the girl with the pyramid jacket had come in and ordered a six-course dinner and, as soon as she got her check, had planted a gigantic cockroach on some fat woman at the next table, and the woman had started screaming and Aida had thought Gunny's was going to get turned in to the Board of Health, and in all the commotion the girl had gotten away without paying for her six-course dinner! And then Nick and his wife had gone to the movies and seen the very same gimmick played on a waiter in a restaurant in Paris. And Nick had sworn if he ever ran into the broad with the pyramid jacket again he would throw her out on her ass.

"Like I always say," Nick said, "violence on the screen leads to violence in the streets."

"Ain't it the truth," the cops said.

Wayne Nolan peeked over his E-Man comic and listened to this story carefully. From the scuffed floor of Gunny's, he rescued the forgotten Magic Club postcard.

Wayne had not slept all night long. He was feeling very tired. But it had all been worth it in the end because now he knew the next place to find Bruce's girl, Susan.

■　□　■

At nine o'clock on Friday morning, when Crystal was arriving to rehearse for a job she would soon not have anymore and Dez was being awakened by Cat on his shoulder, the cops found Roberta's car. No one had stolen it. No splendid new radio had ever been installed in it. The car came back to Gary in perfect condition.

"What do you think she was doing at Battery Park, Mr. Glass?" the cops asked.

Gary couldn't imagine.

His sister, Leslie, recalled something about Roberta reading a message in The Personals that mentioned Battery Park. The cops smiled knowingly. "Lovers often send messages through The Personals," they said.

Gary groaned.

Leslie clucked and sighed.

Becky Shuman called.

"Get out of my brother's life, you greedy bitch," Leslie growled at her.

Gary overheard this conversation, but he did nothing to prevent it. His secretary and his tub salesmen knew about Roberta's disappearance now; Larry Stillman's patients knew; the news was all over Fort Lee and spreading across the Meadowlands; his reputation was already ruined, so what the hell?

Abandoned; betrayed; hungry.

Thank God he had his car back at least.

He waited at home for further word of Roberta. Although the police were quite sure she had run off with her phantom lover, there was still the vivid possibility that she might have been murdered. So when his in-laws called from Florida, Gary lied and said she was out having brunch with the girls. When Roberta's mother called from the Swiss Alps, he lied and said she was out shopping.

"Don't lie to me, Gary," Roberta's mother said. (She sounded as though she were around the corner.) "Roberta does not go shopping. Tell me the truth."

"She's left me," he said.

"Are you sure?"

"No, I'm not. All I know is we can't find her."

Roberta's mother hung up. Gary could just see her dumping her skis and her newest boyfriend and taking the next plane. He groaned. Between his kid sister, Leslie, and Roberta's mother, he figured *he* would be dead by the time they found out that Roberta wasn't.

He sat in the living room, watching the stock market returns on TV. Daisy the Great cleaned around him. He lifted his feet when she wanted to vacuum. He changed chairs when she wanted to plump pillows. Other than that, he did not move all day.

Leslie called. Larry Stillman called. Gary's secretary called. The German hot-tub salesman and Adrian from the beauty parlor and some total stranger from the dry cleaner's all called to find out if there was any word on Roberta.

But the police did not call.

They were very busy.

They had murders. They had bank robberies. They also had a terrible problem keeping the press from realizing that they had no leads, not even one, as to the whereabouts of the Egyptian artifacts that had been heisted from the Brooklyn Museum.

The mayor held a press conference. "My fellow New Yorkers," he said, "fill up your refrigerators, because if the cops don't find the Nefertiti earrings soon, the Egyptian Third Army is gonna overrun our city, and you know how they can eat!"

Then the fake earrings started to pour in, just as Mr. Baloney had predicted.

"I found these earrings in a junk shop on Lower Broadway," Victoria said to the curator of the Cairo Museum, who was now installed at MOMA.

"Like hell you did," said the curator. "But you are a beautiful woman and a talented smelter. Why don't we have lunch?"

■   □   ■

Wayne Nolan lurked outside the Magic Club, hiding in shadows. He left messages with Mr. Baloney's machine. But no courier came.

He bought a *Morning Downer* and scoured it for any mention of his name or Bruce's, but clearly the *Downer* found news of the Great Queen of Egypt Caper unfit to print. He bought the New York *Mirror* in the afternoon. Sure enough, there was Bruce's picture.

"Police are looking for Meeker's ex-partner," the paper said, "both in connection with the murder and, it is widely reported, in connection with the theft of Egyptian artifacts. . . ."

Wayne called Mr. Baloney again.

The operator told him that the number had been disconnected.

Wayne sank onto the pavement next to the derelict. Now he was really scared.

Abandoned; betrayed; hungry.

He recalled how quickly the clumsy oaf who had dropped the Fragonard on his toes had disappeared, probably buried in a reservoir in Jersey, never to be found again. Wayne feared that the same fate awaited him if he did not find the earrings.

He thought of following Bruce's girl, Susan, into the club. But the bullet holes in the door gave him pause; the people in there obviously had automatic weapons. He would have to wait. He glanced at the derelict. Lucky old wino, who had nothing to fear, who could just close his eyes and stretch out . . . and sleep. . . .

■   □   ■

Gary stayed awake by concentrating on a breaking report that the smallest bank in St. Louis had suddenly cut its prime rate by a full percentage point. Not taking his eyes off the screen, he heated up a TV dinner. It had fried chicken and mashed potatoes, two of his favorite but lately most forbidden foods. Roberta's mother called. "I'm in the Zurich airport," she said. "There's a rock blockade and my plane is delayed. Page me if you hear any news."

Suddenly Gary dropped the phone. Daisy the Great was leaving and carrying a pink shopping bag he had seen before. It said "Love Saves the Day" on it. "That's where she bought the jacket!" Gary yelled. "Where did you get this bag, Daisy?"

"Gary? Gary, are you there?" asked Roberta's mother from Zurich.

"It's mine," Daisy said. "Mrs. Glass gave it to me."

"Daisy, give me the bag."

Daisy shook her head sadly. "Sorry," she said.

"Give me the bag!"

Gary was trying to wrench the shopping bag from Daisy.

"Gary!" screamed Roberta's mother. "What's happening?"

How could Gary know that last Wednesday when Roberta had given her the shopping bag, Daisy had found $500 in the street and her husband, Jesus, had returned to her, *sober* yet, begging forgiveness after three years' absence, and her son, Enrique, had gotten a *job*, a real job yet, with Workmen's Comp, as an all-night watchman in a storage facility on Lower Broadway, and that all this good fortune Daisy attributed to the acquisition of the pink shopping bag, which did actually say "Love Saves the Day," something Daisy now believed with all her heart. "You ain't getting this," she said to Gary Glass.

"Please, Daisy, please. I'm asking you nicely."

"Nossir, I'm sorry, no way."

Gary pulled the television out of the wall and held it aloft. "You want me to throw this at your head, Daisy?"

"I tell you what I do, I loan you the bag, Mr. Glass, okay?"

Gary put down the television.

"Thank you."

"But you got to give it back to me Monday," Daisy added, "or I call up my son, Enrique, who's been arrested three times for aggravated battery, and he will come take it by force, you got that, Mr. Glass? I hope you have good news about Mrs. Glass," she said.

"Thank you," he said.

Meanwhile, in Zurich, a young French archeology professor became concerned because the American woman in the phone booth next to him was screaming, "Gary, you putz! Answer me!"

The Frenchman thought she was very attractive and probably needed a drink. As he hung up her phone, he heard a television in Fort Lee saying, "This is the lowest the prime rate has gone in almost ten years and should guarantee the reelection of a Republican administration."

"Merde," said the Frenchman.

"Shit," said Gary, because when he pulled up in front of Love Saves the Day, three mean-looking motorcycle freaks immediately sat on his car, and they were eating pizza(!) and drinking beer(!).

"Hey, guys, could you have your picnic somewhere else?" Gary said sternly. They looked up at him with murder in their eyes.

"Well, just try to be careful, all right?" He hoped for better luck inside.

"I don't get involved in domestic disputes," "Tina Turner" said.

"There's no dispute!" Gary cried. "She was wearing the jacket when she disappeared. It was very special to her for some reason. You've got to remember the jacket."

"Vaguely," "Tina" answered.

"Great," said Gary. "Thanks. You've been a terrific help." He assumed that open-mouthed, beaten-dog look of bitter disappointment that had so pissed off Roberta. This time it worked. "Tina's" heart softened.

"Wait a minute," "Tina" said. "Look, this broad

stopped by looking for the jacket, too. Here's her phone number. Maybe you can help each other."

Susan was studying her map of Egypt and listening to the Fixx sing "One Thing Leads to Another" when the phone rang, and one thing led to another, and she agreed to meet Gary Glass at Rocketeria on West Twenty-first Street at ten-thirty that night.

"Who was it?" asked Crystal. She wiggled her toes. She had painted her toenails black. She thought they looked nice. "Another one of your secret admirers?"

"He says he's the witch's husband," said Susan. "He calls himself Gary Glass. It's obviously an alias. Nobody has a name like that."

■　□　■

Roberta couldn't believe it, but she was going onstage! No sooner had she walked into the Magic Club—such a nice, clean place, so recently mopped!—than this lovely woman offered her coffee and a Twinkie and this nice man with white bucks and a blue leisure suit offered her a job!

Well, why not? she figured. How far does a hundred dollars go in the Big Apple? Dez O'Herlihy seemed determined to get rid of her, so she would have to find another place to live. Of course she needed a job, and since she had no idea what jobs she had ever held before, magician's assistant sounded great.

Henry and Max and Vito, these three perfectly darling old gentlemen in the band, made her comfortable and told her not to be nervous, and the handsome young emcee gave her a pink-and-gray tutu to wear, which she just loved! And to top it off, there were birds in the act! A cute, fuzzy duck and a pair of mellow doves, all fluttery.

This guy Ian the magician was really talented. He could make bunches of flowers come out of his pockets. He could make birds disappear with a wave of his wand. He gave Roberta a name—Davina, Queen of the Night. She *loved* that name. She felt it suited her.

All afternoon they rehearsed. It helped immeasurably that every time she tripped or dropped something, Kaminsky the dummy cried out from the wings: "Don't worry, Susan, you'll have the hang of it by the time the audience gets here, and, even if you don't, it won't matter because this audience is very easily satisfied!"

"Tell that dummy to shut up!" Ian yelled. (A ventriloquist with dirty nails and dandruff locked Kaminsky in the suitcase, to Roberta's disappointment.)

The hardest job was getting dressed.

While Wonder Woman and Claudette Colbert looked on pityingly, Roberta tried to stuff her breasts into the tutu. They kept coming out. "Gilda!" she called. "Could you come here a minute? I think this tutu is too small!"

"Not so, my child," said Gilda. "You're just being modest. At the Magic Club, it's better to let it all hang out."

"All?" asked Roberta. "I mean, *all?*"

Still, Roberta remained concerned. She put on the blonde wig that sat on the Styrofoam head in the dressing room and hung her big gold earring from it, admiring the effect. Ray the manager was already onstage, welcoming the audience.

"Better get out there, sweetheart," said Kaminsky. "Showtime."

Still stuffing herself back into the tutu, Roberta clomped onstage. Ian was a little mad at her.

"From now on I want you here five minutes before the act begins, Susan."

"This tutu doesn't fit, Ian."

"Remember, we start with the doves."

"I'm very worried about embarrassing you in front of all these nice people. . . ."

"You look beautiful. Now smile!"

The band played a chord. The audience clapped. (How many people are out there? Roberta wondered. Eight? Ten?) The curtain went up in a puff of smoke. Roberta coughed and gagged. When she could see again, she saw that, yes, there were about ten people in the audience.

Henry played a waltz on the saxophone; Vito scratched the snares. Trying to remember her moves, Roberta picked up an empty bird cage from the little prop table. Ian tapped it with his butterfly net. Poof! A bird appeared inside!

"Wow, that's terrific!" Roberta marveled. Ian hit the bird cage again. Another dove appeared.

"Way to go!" chirped Roberta.

Ian leaned in very close to her so the audience wouldn't hear him whisper, "Calm down, Susan, you're not a guest here. You're *performing!*"

"Right, right," she said, "sorry . . ." and she ran to get him the multicolored scarf from the prop table. When she bent over to pick up the scarf, her whole chest fell out of the tutu. Luckily she was facing up-stage. Only Kaminsky saw.

She adjusted her costume and handed the scarf to

Ian. With one twist of his hand, he made it produce yet another dove!

"Oooh, I love that!" Susan exclaimed.

Ian gave her a dirty look, but the audience actually applauded. Ian turned over the dove to Susan. Despite her afternoon's training, it got away and flew into the rafters above a guy who looked like Burt Reynolds, sort of.

"Oh, come back!" cried Roberta, bouncing off the stage and jiggling among the tables. "Come back, please!"

For the first time in the history of the Magic Club, the entire audience woke up. "Burt Reynolds" ran after Roberta, trying to help her catch the dove. "Menthol," said the wraithlike cigarette girl, "extra-long, ultrathin, extraultralong and thin, regular, premium . . ."

"I got him!" yelled "Burt Reynolds."

". . . unleaded . . ."

"Oh thank you, sir!" cried Davina, Queen of the Night.

The band played *two* chords! The audience cheered!

"Susan!" Ian whispered. "The platter!"

Clutching the dove to her cleavage, Roberta ran back onstage and stashed the dove and, quick, grabbed the silver platter. The band played Vienna waltzes. Trying to be calm, like Dez, Roberta approached a very old guy and a very young girl, obviously his daughter, Roberta thought. (Maybe it's her birthday. She's gonna love this trick!) Carefully, she placed the platter on the table. Ian followed her and deftly removed the cover. Nothing there. An empty platter, right? Vito did a drum roll. All ten customers got tense. Ian lit a match and the platter burst into flames.

"Aghhh!" cried the young girl.

"Aghhh!" croaked the old man.

Ian grabbed a napkin and put out the fire, and lo, what was born in the flames like a phoenix? A duck!

"Oooh, I love it, I love it, I love it!" Roberta exclaimed.

The young girl was so delighted with this wonderful trick that she kissed her daddy full on the mouth, which was an odd thing for a daughter to do, but what the hell, anything can happen in show biz! Roberta grabbed the duck. He flew away like his dove cousin. By now the audience thought bird losing was part of the act.

"Get that duck back, Susan!" Ian hissed.

Off she went, plunging and tripping among the customers. "Burt Reynolds" joined in the chase; two Cuban sisters who hadn't had a night out in years joined in; the sugar daddy and his birthday girl joined in; squawk, went the duck. "Jesus Christ," Ray groaned backstage.

"Like my mother always told me, Ray," commented Kaminsky, "if you bring home a turkey, you can't expect her to know how to cook a duck."

The only customer who didn't help in the duck hunt was Wayne Nolan. (He had not been moved to help Susan restore her fallen stuff to the drum case, and he was not going to run after her duck now.) He sat tight in his shadow. He watched the large golden earring on Roberta's wig. Queen Nefertiti's blue glass eyes flashed at him. He continued drinking brandy on an empty stomach. His suit was dusty, and his unshaven face was grim with whiskers. They were coming in gray. His hands trembled. Ian the magician brushed past him, holding the duck and dragging Bruce's girl, Susan, back up onto the stage. The audience was cheering.

Ian bowed. Bruce's girl, Susan, remembered that she was supposed to bow, too, so she bowed. The curtain came down with a thump, grazing her nose and hitting her in the chest. There went the tutu!

"Nice try, kid," said Ray. "Here's twenty bucks. We'll see you tomorrow night, same time."

"You're hiring me?"

"Of course we're hiring you."

"Oh thanks, that's great! Thanks, Ray! Gee!"

Ray handed her the duck and the two doves in their cage. "Now, you take these guys home, okay, and you practice, okay?"

"Oooh, I'm so excited! I love show business!"

"Susan . . ."

"What?"

"Practice *a lot.*"

Roberta ran excitedly to the ladies' dressing room. She took a swig of the scotch that was sitting on the long counter—it belonged, in fact, to Gilda, who knocked on its comforting door every half hour or so. Her wig she left on the Styrofoam head, with the long gold earring still attached. "You're my lucky earring," she crooned. "You're gonna make me a star."

Tonight, she figured, Dez would let her sleep under the fish tank again. Tomorrow she would return to the Magic Club to rehearse the Lady-in-the-Coffin trick, and she would practice with her birds and be wonderful! Also she would look for a place of her own, because Dez was a good friend, but how much can you impose on your friends?

She pulled on her pyramid jacket and hit the streets. She had never felt happier in her whole life.

But hers was a fleeting high. The streets were very dark outside the Magic Club.

All around, the warehouses lay low, like muggers. Their dark, dirty windows showed no spark of life. Roberta knew that Broadway was someplace around here, but she didn't know precisely where. The doves cooed; the duck slept, providing no company; and she found it hard to walk on the crumbling pavement with her high heels.

She turned a corner. No Broadway. She turned back and found herself in an alley. It stank of piss and garbage. She heard something behind her and turned. A cat with porcupine hair arched its long back and hissed and did not flinch.

Surely Broadway must be at the end of this alley. She began to hurry, afraid that the cat would attack her birds, afraid of hungry things in the night. It seemed to take her a very long time to get to the end of the alley. Broadway was not there. But she heard strange, squeaky footsteps behind her, and now she began to run.

The alley led into another alley, and when Roberta turned the corner, she found herself face to face with a fire. It crackled in a trash can, emitting cinders. Who set the fire? A wino maybe, a nice, harmless, friendly wino, but where was he? She looked and looked, but there was no wino, just decaying brick walls that dripped like the inside of a tomb. She ran around another corner and leaned against the wall, out of breath. Still the footsteps kept coming. She peeked around the black, craggy wall. The light of the fire revealed the blond hair of a man she felt she had seen somewhere before.

She ran gasping up the alley, beating on windows, looking for a door, a gate, looking for Broadway, a wino, anything to save her from the shifty, shuffling footsteps of the sluggish man who was chasing her. "Please," she whimpered, banging on doors. "Please, please . . ."

One of them opened.

She found herself in the security room of a warehouse, stumbling over mops and plungers, almost crashing into a wall of packaged light bulbs.

Enrique looked up from his big, bloody roast beef sandwich. He stopped watching the big redheaded Spanish singer dancing half naked on the tube. Another half-naked woman was standing in his mop-lined hallway, breathing hard and holding birds.

"Excuse me, sir," Roberta stammered. "I'm sorry to disturb your dinner, but I need you for a second. There's, uh, there's, uh, this man following me. I know he's . . . uh . . . he's out there, running after, uh, me. . . . Couldn't you please . . ."

"How did you get in here?" marveled Enrique. "You are not supposed to be in here."

"Oh I know, and I'm sorry, I'm really sorry, but could you please see . . . could you please see if he's gone?"

As far as Enrique was concerned, the appearance of Roberta in this disgusting hole (where he was grateful to be working after three convictions for aggravated battery) was akin to the appearance of Jesus to St. Theresa. He crossed himself and devoutly thanked God.

"Okay, I go see," he said, looking at Roberta's legs, her breasts, her birds.

"Thank you," she said, panting.

"You stay here," Enrique commanded.

"Yes, yes, I stay here."

"Enrique will take care of everything."

He grinned. He said a little prayer. Before he left, he took one last look at her legs. He went off whistling and crossing himself and licking his chops in the manner of Cat.

Roberta sagged into Enrique's broken spring chair. It dropped a foot and tipped her over backward, right into a calendar that displayed the insides of women's bodies. (This calendar was so shocking to Roberta that at first she didn't even realize what she was looking at.) Horrified, she swung upward quickly and flipped herself forward into the bloody red roast beef sandwich. She got ketchup on her nose. She thought she might barf on the sandwich.

"*¡Hola!*" said a strange television personality on Enrique's television. "*¡Soy Gary, de Gary's Oasis!*"

Roberta peered at the personality. What an odd-looking man he was, with his safari suit and his pith helmet, with all those silly, giggling girls splashing and frolicking around him! He kept babbling in Spanish, and suddenly the girls pulled him into the water. "*¡No, muchachas, no!*" he yelled.

An announcer who had a Spanish accent like Billy Crystal came on the air. "At Gary's Oasis," he said, "all your fantasies come troooo!"

Roberta searched her memory. Why did she feel she had been to Gary's Oasis? Was it a luncheonette, like Gunny's? Was it a disco, or a club, someplace she hung out with Jim? Why would she and Jim go someplace where people dressed up in such funny clothes and then went swimming? The sound of the elevator brought her back to reality. She heard clanging doors, being locked for the night by Enrique, so that no burglar could break in and disturb his miraculous assignation with the beautiful bird girl delivered into his hands by the Blessed Virgin and all the saints.

Somehow Roberta knew that staying here was probably not the smartest thing she could do. She had a choice between Enrique and the alley. She chose the alley.

Outside again, she listened. Nothing. She looked. No blond guy. She hurried down the alley and turned a corner. There, before her, lay a well-lit street with passersby and music and open stores! Roberta ran toward it gasping, "Broadway, Broadway!"

A taxi flashed yellow as a sunrise, ignoring her shrieks as it passed. No matter. She knew she was going to be okay now. All she had to do was run, run (her heart felt as though it would explode). All she had to do was find a taxi, stay in the light, get past these ruins, these bombed-out, burned-out, gutted buildings that looked as though they were left over from a war. She turned to look behind her, but the man wasn't there and Enrique wasn't there, and soon another taxi would pass, and she would be okay and she would go home to Dez . . . no, Jim . . . no, Dez with the angel blue eyes and the fish tank, and the heel of her shoe caught in a cobblestone and her heel broke, and she tripped and staggered, and Wayne Nolan grabbed her.

She screamed.

An iron hand locked over her mouth. An arm like a girder locked around her waist. She kicked and thrashed, but she couldn't get away. The man was tearing at the shopping bag that contained her clothes.

"Don't scream," the man whispered, letting his fingers up off her mouth.

"Don't kill me!"

"Let's get this over with. Where are they?"

"Wait, wait, wait, I have money!"

"Where are they?"

"In my bag I have money. Take it. Oh God . . ."

"I want the earrings," he whispered. He was dragging her back into the hole he had come out of. He smelled musty, like the inside of an old, damp car.

"What earrings?" she cried.

"I need them."

"What earrings? Look, I'm not who you think . . . please, please . . ."

He locked his hand over her mouth again and put a gun to her head. The safety clicked off, a thunderous sound. Roberta's heart stopped. She said hello to the angel of death coming to announce the end of her life. All she saw was his smile; the rest of him remained invisible. "Robertaaaaa," he said, "Robertaaaa."

"All right, all right," the musty mugger mumbled, "avoid the fate of your late, beloved boyfriend. . . ."

Roberta started to faint. She saw flashing red lights. The mugger with the iron hands dropped her and grabbed her shopping bag and vanished into a black hole. She fell down and down as though she had been dropped into a reservoir. By the time her head hit bottom, she had already passed out.

When she opened her eyes, a cop was standing above her, shining a big flashlight into her face.

"Was he your pimp?" said the cop to Roberta.

"What?"

"All right, play it that way if you want. Come on, sweetheart, you've just got a little bump on your head. You'll survive it." He pulled her to her feet. She didn't know where she was. Her head pounded and roared and hurt like hell. "What's your name?" he asked.

"I don't know."

"Get in the car."

He pushed her in the back seat of a police car that was flashing its red lights up and down Broadway. A black woman was already in the car.

"My name's Roberta," Roberta said suddenly.

The cop shut her into the car with the other woman, tight as meat in a sandwich.

"I'm not who you think I am!" Roberta cried against the window. "My name is Roberta! My name is Roberta!" She beat on the window. My God, she thought, I am wearing fingerless gray lace gloves! She beat her head against the glass. "My name is Roberta Glass!"

Her head hurt so much, throbbed so powerfully, that she had to hold it to keep it from falling off. When she looked at her fingers, there was blood.

"How do you use the birds?" asked the real whore who was sitting next to her, with considerable interest.

Chapter 5

Gary Glass took a lot of pride in his ability to catch on quickly and make friends in strange places. At the Wharton School, which he attended as a lower-middle-class kid on scholarship, a fraternity filled with the sons of millionaires accepted Gary gladly because he glibly ghosted all their economics papers. In four years, he almost never paid for a meal or a beer, and at graduation, everybody felt as though they owed him.

As a young man just starting out in his father's plumbing business, he had been called upon to attend many ethnic festivities that were, his father said, a necessary part of the big picture in sales. Gary always dressed well, brought the right presents, and laid out the women with his boyish charm. The mother of the bride at a Serbo-Croatian wedding in Cleveland told his father that Gary was a credit to his race. The sister of the groom at a Black church in Brooklyn liked the way Gary pushed her grandmother's wheelchair from table to table at the reception, so Gramma could personally greet each of the guests.

"You trying to look like hired help, sugar?" asked the lovely granddaughter.

"I don't care what I look like as long as your grandmother lets me take you to dinner," Gary said.

This did a lot to help Glass Plumbing win the contract for bathrooms in a five-thousand-unit housing project way up on the West Side, and to make it a much bigger business.

Gary admired his father more than any person in the entire world. He was a tough cookie. He had nerves of plastic. In all things, he was wise. "You can worry about health; you can worry about money; you can worry about politics," Daddy said. "But for God's sake, don't worry about women; there's too many other things to worry about."

The first great turning point in Gary's life occurred when he and his father attended a major exhibition of sinks, pipes, and bathtubs in Frankfurt. They checked into a nice hotel, with many other businessmen from New York. To Gary's astonishment, he found that his father, the tough cookie, was afraid to take a shower in this place, and couldn't eat, and certainly couldn't sleep, and in the middle of the night, he returned to the airport, where he sat with many other businessmen from New York, waiting for the next plane out.

Gary stayed in Frankfurt. He drank the beer; he ate the wurst; he did the deals; he became intimate with the women. His father met him at Kennedy, beaming and proud. "The torch has been passed to a new generation," he said, giving Gary a big hug.

When Gary upgraded the plumbing-supply business to spas and hot tubs, his father had already had one heart attack and wanted little to do with the wining and dining requisite for such a tremendous expansion. "Go and conquer the world, kid," he said. "It's full of thieves and anti-Semites, but if you keep your head and marry a shy, repressed woman you can trust, you just may survive."

Gary's father died in his sleep.

Now Roberta had disappeared.

Gary began to feel that some of his bedrock was slipping. It wasn't Roberta; she could hardly be called bedrock. It was the wisdom of the fathers, most particularly his father, which seemed suddenly to rest, like the city of Los Angeles, on a colossal fault.

He put these thoughts from his mind. He endured the psychoanalytic outrages of the police. He suffered street people eating lunch on his beautiful car. He softened the heart of "Tina Turner." Determined and courageous, confident that he could handle any situation no matter how bizarre, he set out for Rocketeria on West Twenty-first Street to meet this strange woman called Susan.

And the earthquake happened.

Gary Glass felt that he had fallen through a crack in the earth's crust and landed in a world inhabited by subterranean aliens. He steadied himself against a wall. Four ash-colored people with pink hair on their heads and diamond dust on their faces danced past him; he couldn't tell whether they were male or female. Beyond them the big pink room was packed with people who writhed and shimmied, and the music, which Gary had picked up before on radios but never *listened* to, boomed and ground and rocked.

Calm yourself, Glass. These are not subterraneans, he thought of the crowd, these are Americans like you. They just have different habits. You can make friends with anyone.

A zombie with no hair and with rainbows around his eyes danced by with a female in a sheet. Don't panic, Gary said to himself. There must be some groove here you can get into. All you have to do is dance like the others. It can't be too hard. No one seems really hostile. Stay calm.

He took a step forward. A black jellyfish girl with Medusa hair and with snakes around her arms thought he wanted to dance; she threw her hair in his face and writhed and laughed. Maybe I ought to take off my tie, Gary said to himself.

A woman old enough to be Mommy placed herself in front of Gary and blew smoke in his face, glancing inquisitively at his three-piece suit. She smiled seductively. She had gold teeth with silver braces on them. She's gonna eat me, Gary thought. She's gonna eat my suit.

Something in the music told him he had better move. Up ahead, beyond the dozens of smoking, sniffing, rocking people (none of whom was talking; these people have forgotten how to speak, Gary thought, after all their long years underground), he saw a regular human bar with regular human drinks and a bartender.

The bartender wore a leather vest and a leather jock strap with a big butterfly stuck to it. Otherwise he was completely naked. But he had a real human body, so Gary decided to put one foot in front of the other and walk toward him. He could not really walk, though, because the speakers that were mounted on the floor as well as on the ceiling banged music into the soles of his feet, so even Gary had to dance slightly to get to the bar.

Gary had forgotten why he was there. He saw a juke box. A real human juke box. I am at Rocketeria on West Twenty-first Street, he said to himself, that's where I am, and I am looking for a woman who can help me find my wife, Roberta, who has disappeared. I am not here to sell hot tubs. I am not here . . .

"Gary Glass, right?"

She was gorgeous.

"Yeah, how did you know?"

"Wild guess," Susan said.

She was absolutely gorgeous, even though she was clearly not a regular human being.

"She split on you, huh?" she said.

Gary couldn't take his eyes off her belly button. It nestled in its black lace frame like a diamond in a case at Cartier. It was the most gorgeous belly button he had ever seen in his whole life. Now she had just said something to him and he was going to have to respond. . . .

"What did you say?" he said.

"She split on you. Your wife."

"Oh yes, right, of course, my wife, uh, two days ago."

Her bra was showing. He could see her black lace bra! Why had he never noticed bras before?

"Did she ever split on you before?"

Think, Gary, he said to himself. Concentrate. This beautiful bra . . . broad . . . woman is talking to you in English. She has asked you whether your wife . . .

what was her name? . . . Oh yes, Roberta . . . whether your wife, Roberta, ever left before.

"No, uh, no, of course not."

"Did she do drugs?" the belly button asked. She had black-and-gold-striped hair and one gigantic earring—what a gorgeous earring!

"Drugs? Roberta?" Gary laughed. He had this vision of Roberta sniffing lines in the ladies' room of this pink place. It was such a funny idea that it brought him back to reality. "Roberta never smoked a joint in her life," he said. "She's probably the straightest person in Fort Lee."

The gorgeous woman smiled and put her little pink tongue through the space between her front teeth. "Oh yeah?" she said. Clearly she did not believe him about Roberta. What was she, another cop?

"Look, what are you driving at?" Gary said, trying to sound offended but really her dazzling earring was making him perspire. She offered him something to drink. He was afraid that if he had a drink, he would pass out and be trampled to death by the gyrating green-haired people.

"Oh, uh, no, thank you. I'm on this health program, you know, no, uh, no alcohol, no sugar, no salt."

"You wanna dance?"

Oh my God, he thought, she has asked me to dance. If I dance, I'll get dizzy and fall down and I will be trampled to death by the gyrating blue-haired people. "Sure . . . sure, let's dance . . ." he said, and then she turned her back to him and lifted her plump, firm, white arms, which had black rubber fan belts around them, and she shook her body. She is dancing, Gary thought. Her name is Susan, and she knows where Roberta is, and I must dance with her. I must, I must, I must dance, even though I will not be able to sell her a hot tub.

Gary danced. Sort of. A girl in kelly-green tights intruded between him and Susan and danced with him. A white-haired man in black leather danced with Susan. Gary bumped into half a dozen other people.

"Excuse me," he said. "Oh, uh, excuse me."

Susan turned to face him. Her belly button was moving from side to side like a bouncing ball.

"Did you read that stuff in the newspaper about that guy Meeker? He got pushed out of a hotel window in Atlantic City."

Concentrate on what she's saying, Gary said to himself. Do not concentrate on the bouncing ball.

"Roberta's mixed up in it," she said.

Roberta! Pushed out a window! In Atlantic City! No no, that's not what she said. . . . *What had she said?*

"You have the wrong Roberta," he protested. "My Roberta could not possibly be mixed up in a hotel window, I mean . . ."

"It's a fact," said Susan, bouncing. "She is trying to frame me for Meeker's murder."

And then Susan disappeared.

"Wait a minute, wait a minute. . . . Who's Meeker?" Gary yelled. A zombie came and danced with him. I do not want to dance with a zombie, Gary thought. Then he turned around.

Susan was behind him. She had diamonds on her boots. No, that's impossible, nobody has diamonds on their boots, Gary thought.

"Who's Meeker, and what does he have to do with Roberta?"

"His ex-partner and Roberta were in on it together."

"I, uh, I think really you must be mistaken. Roberta doesn't know anybody in Atlantic City."

Or does she? he thought.

Maybe Roberta has a black bra and a bouncing belly button and diamonds on her boots, too, but I, Gary, have never seen them because Roberta keeps them in a hotel in Atlantic City.

"I saw Roberta and Meeker's ex-partner together," Susan said.

Oh my God, it's true, the cops are right. Roberta is seeing another man. No, that is impossible, Gary thought. "No, that is impossible," Gary said.

"He looks like a real greaseball to me," Susan commented, before disappearing again.

Greaseball? thought Gary. A female with Saran Wrap shorts . . . no, it was a man . . . no, it was a woman . . . shook her thin hips at Gary, and Gary shook his thin hips at her . . . no, him . . . no . . . thinking: Roberta hates grease; all her pans are Teflon, she never fries fish; she never sautés onions; I am a totally greaseless man, and yet Roberta hugs and kisses me. . . . Susan came back.

"I don't believe a word you're saying!" Gary proclaimed.

Susan danced a little closer. She put her hand on Gary's arm, burning a hole in his suit (Gary was quite sure of that). "Gar," she said, "trust me." (She has called me "Gar," he thought. That's a sign that she likes me!) "You want to find your wife?"

No, no, he thought, I don't want to find my wife. I want this gorgeous woman to burn holes in all my suits and bounce her belly button at me forever!

"Of course I want to find my wife," he said.

"Good," concluded Susan. "Let's go to your place."

Whoopie! thought Gary. I did it! I fell into a subterranean cavern where the zombies dance, and I made friends!

"My place?" he said innocently, but he wasn't really surprised. The famous, marvelous Glass charm had won out again.

"You got a car?" she asked.

"Have I got a car!" said Gary. He loosened his tie and took off his jacket and drove her to Fort Lee.

But no sooner did they arrive in his fully electronic, automatic, digital garage than Gary got nervous again. What if somebody saw them? Here he is, the object of sympathy and pity throughout the town because his wife, Roberta, has disappeared, and the second night she is gone, he shows up with a gorgeous woman in black lace with one earring!

Calm down, Gary, he told himself, it's three o'clock in the morning, the neighbors' windows are all dark, and, besides, according to Roberta's reports from the beauty parlor, there is so much lechery, adultery, sodomy, and litigation going on here that everybody else is probably too busy with their own amusements to pay attention to you.

Susan gave herself a little spray with the cologne Roberta kept on the front-hall table. It was really the first time Gary had noticed that cologne. He wondered whether Roberta ever sprayed herself with it. Maybe she sprayed the light bulbs with it and that was why the house smelled so good all the time. In fact, it was the first time Gary had ever noticed that the house really did smell good.

Susan trailed her fingers along the furniture tops, drifting lanquidly from room to room and smiling. Gary followed her, waiting for the moment when she would drift languidly over him, too. Thank God Daisy was here today, he thought to himself. What if Susan had trailed her fingers over something that had dust on it? But nothing had dust on it, thank God. For the first time, Gary thought to himself that Daisy was really a great maid and should probably get a raise, although he had no idea what Roberta was paying her now. Maybe she was already overpaid. He made a mental note to ask Roberta about that, if she ever came home. . . . Oh God, he hoped she would not come home tonight.

"Nice place you got here, Gar," Susan said.

"We like it," he said.

Why did I say that? he thought. "We," why did I say "we"? Am I trying to remind her that Roberta lives here, too? Maybe I am.

She drifted into the bedroom.

Gary tried to stay calm.

She sat down on the bed and bounced on it; she stretched out on it; she relaxed on it.

Oh my God, Gary thought.

"Firm," said Susan

You said it, Gary thought. He got ready to jump her.

But then she bounced up and investigated the closet. Roberta's closet. Gary had never actually been in Roberta's closet; he assumed she had clothes in there and shoes and whatever else she wore. Susan leafed through the clothes and put on a black sequined jacket that she liked.

"That's Roberta's," Gary said.

"Right," Susan said.

"Now wait a minute, Susan," he said, "don't you think you ought to wait until Roberta gets here before you start taking her clothes?"

"She owes me a coat," Susan said.

She sat down on the bed and began opening the drawers of Roberta's dresser. Gary was beginning to feel uncomfortable. What if Roberta kept something *valuable* in her dresser?

Susan took out a pair of underpants. They were pink lace and extremely attractive. Gary could not remember ever seeing Roberta wear those underpants.

"They must be Roberta's," he said.

"Right," she said.

For whom did Roberta Glass wear those underpants? The greaseball in Atlantic City?

Susan pulled out some books. She read the titles.

"How to Be Your Own Best Friend."

Calm yourself, Gary. You have indeed seen those underpants before. You just never concentrated on them. Roberta wears them all the time. There is no greaseball in Atlantic City.

"I'm Okay You're Okay."

Actually, he couldn't remember ever having seen the jacket Susan was wearing which she had taken out of Roberta's closet, although clearly this was Roberta's jacket. All he could ever remember Roberta wearing was shapeless white pajamas.

"*Dr. Ruth's Guide to Good Sex*," Susan read. "Are these books Roberta's, too?"

"I didn't know she read this stuff."

"Between you and me, Gar," Susan said, "what *do* you know about Roberta?"

Gary decided he no longer wanted to jump Susan. She was just a little bit too snide. It was a good thing she was drifting out of the bedroom ("nice wallpaper," she said), because this whole scene in the bedroom and the closet had irritated Gary just a little bit.

Kicking off her diamond-studded boots, Susan stepped on the bathroom scale. "How much does Roberta weigh?"

How much does Roberta weigh? Gary thought. I should know that. I must know that, approximately at least, I *must!* She's my wife! "A hundred and, uh, uh, five? Ten?"

"We're close," Susan said. "Very close."

I have to get this woman out of my house, Gary thought. This is not my kind of woman; she is just too invasive and pushy. I'm going to tell her to leave.

Susan got into the bathtub.

Oh my God, she's going to take a bath!

"Nice tub."

"You like it?"

Susan stretched and relaxed.

"Yes, I like it."

I've got to find a way to turn her off before she turns on the water, Gary thought.

"It's one of our most popular items," he said. "You can install it in any bathroom, it comes in a variety of colors, it fits all standard plumbing fixtures, and increases the resale value of your house or condominium."

That did the trick. Susan did not turn on the water.

"I didn't say I wanted to buy one," she said, laughing.

She had such a pleasant, musical laugh that Gary decided he no longer wanted her to leave.

"You know, Gar, I could get used to a place like this. Do you have any pot?"

Pot, he thought, she wants pot. I'm going to have to admit to her that I don't have any. Oh, this is such a disgrace; a sophisticated, world-traveling man like me should be prepared for any eventuality.

"Usually, um, I keep some around, but, uh, right now I'm, uh, I'm out. You know how it is."

"How about a match?" she said, laughing, and pulled up her pants leg, revealing several joints tucked conveniently into her sock.

Roberta, Gary thought, where are you?

■   □   ■

Gary and Susan were lying head to head on the newly reupholstered chintz built-in sofas. They had shared several joints. They had sipped a lot of vodka. They were very relaxed. Gary was telling Susan how he felt about the meaning of life.

"So then you start to think," he sighed, "what's it all about? The big picture, you know what I mean?"

"Sure I do, Gar."

"I mean . . . there's more to life than making money, right?"

Susan rolled over voluptuously and handed him the joint.

"Yeah," she said.

"I mean, um, uh . . . mmm," he took a long deep drag, "I mean, I know, I really know, there's more to life . . ."

On the table between them, there were jelly beans and pretzels and little licorice lumps and Twinkies and a gigantic imitation-sequoia ashtray filled with Susan's butts, and there were beers, and one of the beers had spilled on a silver-framed picture of Roberta and Gary, taken on the Costa del Sol two years ago. Susan tried to clean off the puddled picture with a tissue, but she was feeling rather weak and languid, and anyway Gary was passing her back the joint.

"You know . . . you know," mused Gary, "you know how all time comes from a single point in the universe? You know what I mean?"

"No," said Susan. "But tell me, tell me, I wanna know. . . ."

"There are things happening in the solar system so far away that we can't even see them."

"Uh . . . huh . . ." sighed Susan. On the table she had found a little robot. It had bees on its antennae. She wound it up and it marched across the pretzels and the jelly beans and the licorice until it reached a beer puddle and hydroplaned and tipped over.

Susan laughed.

Gary laughed.

"I mean, what do the robots and the aliens out there in the solar system care if I am the spa king of New Jersey? I mean, what do they care, Susan? Did you ever think of that?"

Susan giggled.

Gary giggled and giggled.

The phone rang.

"Welcome to Gary's Oasis," Gary sang, "where all your fantasies come troooo. . . ."

"Hello?" Susan said to the phone. "Hello, Glass House." She handed the phone to Gary; it sort of plopped on his face. "Somebody's calling, but nobody's there," she crooned.

Gary cracked up.

"Hello, hello, spa king of New Jersey!" he giggled and gasped into the phone. "Spa king! This is your spa king speaking. Speak up, speak up for spas!"

Susan was so hysterical that she rolled off the sofa and knocked all the beers onto the carpet, where they poured like the waters of Aswan.

"Whoever it was hung up," Gary said. He fell asleep.

A few hours later the phone rang again.

"Spa king of New Jersey!" mumbled Gary Glass. He had been sleeping on the sofa. Susan was sleeping on the floor.

"Mr. Glass, we have your wife," said the police.

"I have no wife," he said. "My wife has left me for a greaseball in Atlantic City."

"She's in jail. She was picked up a little while ago. As soon as we got her prints and her picture, we sent it up to Missing Persons and Sergeant Taskal said she was your wife; her mug shots match her wedding picture."

"Mug shots? Mug shots!"

Gary lunged up from the sofa. He shook his head until his teeth rattled. He ate a mouthful of jelly beans for strength. He called Leslie.

"Larry? Tell Leslie to get dressed. They found Roberta. She's in jail. Don't ask any questions. Call my cardiologist and my nutritionist and put them on alert. I'll pick Les up in five minutes. Bye."

Leaping over the candy-covered beer table, leaping over Susan, Gary tore off his clothes, ran through the shower, and redressed himself in a clean three-piece suit.

"Hey, Gar, what's the problem?" murmured Susan.

"You've got to get out of here."

"But why? I like it here."

"Because my wife, Roberta, is coming home from jail, and I want the house to be nice and clean and dust free, just the way it was when she left it."

"You expect me to clean up this house, Gar?"

"Forget it, Susan. I'll take care of it later. Just go."

"You got any Captain Crunch? What time is it?"

"It's five o'clock in the morning. See the dawn on the Hudson?"

"Let me ask you something, Gar. My mind is a little fuzzy. Did I make it with you?"

"No! No, you did not make it with me! Put that thought out of your mind. It is a fictional thought!"

"Jeez, that's a relief," Susan said, fixing her earring which had gotten all twisted in the night.

"This is no time to be snide, Susan. Now, Roberta has been found, and I am going to get her, and I want you out of here by the time I get back, no trace, no notes, no stray strands of golden hair, no nothing, okay?"

"You got any money, Gar?"

He gave her twenty dollars. She pouted. He gave her three more twenties, and she gave him back one. "I don't want to break you, lover," she said sweetly.

Don't call me lover!" he screamed. "Just leave. Do

you promise me? Susan? Do you promise me you'll leave?"

"First I gotta take a bath in that terrific tub you got, Gar...."

He gave up and ran out the door. Leslie was waiting for him in front of her building. The minute he saw her, he knew it would have been safer if he had stayed in his drug-induced stupor.

"Why is Roberta in jail?" Leslie asked.

"On a prostitution charge."

"Oh, Gary, oh my God . . ."

"What are you, crazy? Do you *believe* that? Just because Roberta is charged with something by a bunch of blue nits, you believe they are *right?*"

"They are not blue nits, Gary, they are professional policemen doing a job."

"All I can say is that she'd better have a good explanation for all this, driving me crazy with anxiety, making me go off my diet...."

"You haven't seen her and already you're yelling. There is no need to do eighty on the West Side Highway, Gary. This is a very old highway, and much of it has already been reduced to rubble...."

"Will you shut up, Leslie?"

"Just hear her side of it before you do anything."

"She could have picked up a phone and called if she was in trouble."

"Gareeeee . . . Gareeeee, calm down, slow down. . . . Oh, look what I found! A big, chunky rhinestone!"

"Give me that!"

"Garee, keep your eyes on the road and your hands on the wheel. It's only a rhinestone. It probably fell off one of the dresses Roberta wears when she goes to New York and plies her trade and lives her other life."

"She does not ply a trade! She has no other life! If you don't shut up, Les, I am going to shove you out the door into the Hudson!"

Leslie, like Daisy the Great, now saw that Gary Glass did have his limits and would, if pushed, consider violence. So she gave him five minutes to calm down. She clicked her nails on her magnificent teeth. She made little tsking sounds with her tongue—tsk, tsk, tsk. She snapped open and snapped closed her chic lizardskin clutch—snap, unsnap, snap, unsnap.

"You know, Gary," she said finally, "this situation is not that uncommon." Tsk, tsk, snap, unsnap, click, click, click. "I read an article last week in the beauty parlor about a woman from Woodmere who turned tricks until midday and then shopped all afternoon. She did it for years before her husband found out."

Gary Glass did not respond right away.

Susan had said Roberta was a murderess. The cops said Roberta was a prostitute. Given a choice, and knowing Roberta as well as he did, Gary figured she was more likely to be a murderess.

"Roberta cannot be a prostitute," he concluded. "She doesn't even like sex that much."

He careened off the highway and whizzed crosstown on Fourteenth Street.

"I have heard," Leslie said (click, click), "that four out of five prostitutes are lesbians."

Gary laughed and ran a stop light. "I think I would know if my wife were a lesbian."

"Why?" asked Leslie. "You didn't know she was a prostitute."

"It's very lucky for you that we have arrived at the police station, Les, because if we were still on the highway, you would be drowning by now."

"Oh, Gareee, Gareee, do you think it makes me happy to tell you these terrible truths? I just think you have got to accept that there is something very unusual going on in your relationship with Roberta. . . ."

They ran past the cops, past the bleeding gang-war survivors, past the lawyers and the muggers.

"Just be calm," Leslie was saying. "Remember, you are a survivor of the Frankfurt plumbing fair."

Sergeant Taskal of Missing Persons was waiting for them. Really he was very glad to see them. They were the nicest people he had met in a long, long time. He felt very bad when he showed them the mug shot of Roberta, her lipstick smeared across her cheek, her black eye makeup smeared so it looked as though she had two black eyes, and the good-looking sister-in-law sank in her chair and whispered, "Oh my God, oh my God . . ."

He called down to the holding tank for Roberta.

But the holding tank told him somebody had already come for her, paid her bail, and taken her away. A man, they said.

"Who was he?" Gary Glass whined. "Who took my wife, Roberta?"

"Boyfriend, pimp, who knows?" said Sergeant Taskal, as gently as he could. "You want a cup of coffee, Mr. Glass? Mrs., uh . . ."

"My sister is no longer married," said Gary Glass meanly.

"Oh my God . . ." murmured Leslie, still gazing at the horrible mug shot of Roberta.

"I have your number, Mr. Glass. Why don't you let me have yours, too, Ms. Glass, so if one of you isn't home . . ."

Leslie looked for a tissue to wipe her tears away. Sergeant Taskal gave her his handkerchief. For the first time in his life, Gary Glass realized that somebody, in this case an NYPD detective, was putting the make on his sister, his crazy, hysterical sister whom he had always thought to be one of the single most unattractive women in the world, desirable to no one, married for her money alone by "that shit," who then dumped her. And now Larry Stillman wanted her and Sergeant Taskal of Missing Persons wanted her, so if that were the case, why shouldn't some greaseball want Roberta, why shouldn't Roberta be a lesbian prostitute who had been turning tricks in New York for years?

The terrible truth sank in at last.

Daddy Glass had been dead wrong.

You did have to worry about women.

■   □   ■

As soon as Gary left, Susan began her vacation. After all, she knew a windfall when it fell.

She actually did clean up all the beer and pretzels and jelly beans and licorice, threw the butts into the trash compactor, and investigated the refrigerator.

It was full, but dull.

She opened every single cabinet until she found

the secret storage place (which she knew all people on diets have) where Gary kept his junk food in case he wanted to cheat. He had jars of jelly beans there, and Cheez Doodles; he had Twinkies and Tam Tam crackers and chocolate-covered granola nuggets. Susan prepared a platter. Then she decided that the yummiest thing to have at five-thirty in the morning was a pink tequila sunrise, so she made herself one, helping herself to all the marvelous mixers and cherries and limes in the minifridge near the liquor cabinet.

She found the laundry room.

It seemed logical to wash her clothes, which were beginning to smell a little too much of New York.

So she popped them all in the big machine, programmed it for dark colors, delicate fabrics, cool wash, cold rinse, and let 'er rip.

Then she looked out the window, and wow! What did she spy? A personal-size swimming pool, entirely private, with fine wines stacked near its comfortable chaises and a portable cassette stereo at the ready and a portable TV, too. "This is better than camp," she thought, and went skinny-dipping. The water was wonderful, really refreshing—not too much chlorine either. It made the tequila sunrise and the Cheez Doodles taste great.

Feeling clean as a girl scout, Susan stretched out on one of the comfy chaises and pointed her body to the risen sun. The radio played her favorites. The nice, crispy Cheez Doodles melted under her tongue. Oooh, this was heaven. Someday Jimmy Riddle was going to make it big, and they'd have a house just like this one, maybe in Malibu, maybe in Louisville, someplace by the water, where you could hear garbage barges tooting by, like here, and you could have a remote for your television, like here, but then the vacation wouldn't be borrowed from Gary Glass or Bruce Meeker, it would be hers and Jimmy's, theirs alone, and it would last forever. . . .

Susan slapped herself hard in the face, knocking a Cheez Doodle out of her mouth. She immediately jumped back in the water and swam ten laps. One little taste of comfort and a girl could go off the deep end completely!

She pressed the remote and flipped on the television, which brought her the early-morning news. Usually Susan made it a point never to get too well acquainted with the news. The news could give you the blues. But, this morning, she had a special interest; she wanted to know if there were any new developments in the murder of Bruce Meeker. And there were.

"The Egyptian artifacts stolen during the Great Queen of Egypt Caper at the Brooklyn Museum were recovered last night," said this light-skinned black woman in a fabulous three-piece suit, "from a toxic waste dump by a reservoir in central New Jersey. The New Jersey Department of Antiquities reports that everything in the heist was found except the fabulous Nefertiti earrings." The earrings came on screen. *Her* earrings. Susan choked on her tequila sunrise.

"Police throughout the metropolitan area are now looking for Wayne Nolan," continued the anchorwoman, "pictured here with his partner, Bruce Meeker, after they were released pending appeal of their conviction on diamond-smuggling charges in

1982. Meeker was found dead in Atlantic City last Monday afternoon. Nolan is still at large. He is now the prime suspect in the Great Queen of Egypt Caper and is believed still to possess the Nefertiti earrings."

There they were. Meeker and Nolan. Surrounded by journalists and grumpy law-enforcement officers. Meeker was smiling for the cameras. Nolan had his pale head down. He was peeking as far as he could under his own ear.

Yucch! Susan thought to herself.

How could Roberta be involved with that icky guy when she had a nice, square, rich, but really very cute husband like Gary to come home to?

Then it dawned on her.

Susan had one of the earrings, and Roberta had to have the other. Maybe quite by accident. Maybe really quite by accident. . . .

■   □   ■

When Leslie and Gary came home at seven o'clock, they found Susan sprawled on the Glass bed, reading Roberta's diary.

"Who is that woman on your bed, Gary, you pig?" Leslie growled.

"Don't get the wrong idea. She's helping me find Roberta."

"Hi," said Susan.

She was wearing one of Gary's ribbed, sleeveless Fruit of the Loom undershirts and a pair of his ice-blue boxer shorts and her white lace tights and her white lace garter belt.

"I told you to be gone by the time I got back! What are you doing here?" Gary blustered.

"I've got good news and bad news," Susan said. "Which do you want to hear first?"

"You said you were going to leave!"

"*You* said I was going to leave."

"Whose underwear is that?"

"Come on, Gar, it's one thing when you don't recognize Roberta's underwear, but when you don't recognize your own, then you are really losing your marbles."

Gary sank down on the bed, utterly defeated. His sister, Leslie, stood with her mouth open, staring.

"Give me the good news first," Gary said wearily.

"Your wife isn't partners with the greaseball."

"Wonderful!" Gary said. "That's wonderful! I'm very glad to hear that! My wife, as you so delicately put it, has just been picked up on the Lower East Side escaping from her gun-toting pimp!"

"He's not a pimp."

"He's not a pimp?"

"Who's not a pimp?" asked Leslie.

"The bad news is that he's probably going to kill her because he thinks she's me."

Leslie began snapping and unsnapping her clutch.

"Will you stop that?" yelled Gary.

"I'm looking for Sergeant Taskal's card. We have to call him. I just can't find it."

"How can you *not* find it? He gave it to you four times!"

Leslie went into the bathroom because she was so frightened for Roberta she was going to cry, and under no circumstances could she allow her brother, Gary, to see that.

"Did you ever see this diary?" Susan asked Gary.

"What?"

"Your wife, Roberta, kept a diary. It's great stuff. You want me to read it? I'll read it. 'Couldn't sleep. Went into kitchen. Gary came in. Turned on light. Gary left. Finished birthday cake.' There are pages and pages just like that. I say it's got to be a cover. Nobody's life could be this boring."

"You shouldn't be reading that," Gary said. "It's private."

"Yeah? Well, it's not only about her, it's also about me. Listen to this. 'He's looking for Susan again. She's late returning from Mexico. This is the fifth ad he's run. Why does he want to see her so badly? Who is she?' "

Gary laughed.

"To tell you the truth, Susan, I would like to know that, too. Who are you? Who the hell are you, and why does my entire life suddenly hinge on what you do?"

"Look," Susan said, walking across the bed on her knees. "Here's my picture." She put her arm around Gary, who was feeling very dejected and much older than he had the night before. "Hey, Gar, now why didn't you tell me she read The Personals?"

Leslie came out of the bathroom.

"She read The Personals all the time," Leslie snapped. "You know that, Gary, you saw her. You saw how she bought the *Mirror* every single day and spent hours looking at The Personals when she knew damn well she should have been reading the want ads."

"I . . . I never thought . . ." Gary said.

"Fortunately for everybody," Susan announced,

"I'm here and I'm thinking. Gary, give me your car keys."

Gary obediently jingled around in his pocket and found them and gave them to Susan. Susan took his previous day's shirt off the back of a chair and put it on over his underwear and her tights and left.

"Gary, are you crazy? You just *gave* her the car keys!" Leslie hissed.

"I'll bring it right back," Susan called from the front door.

"Gareee! You just gave a strange woman dressed in very little else except your underwear the keys to your new black Ford convertible!"

"Just shut up, Leslie, okay?"

He picked up a bag of Cheez Doodles that Susan had been munching on his bed, and it opened and spilled all over the pink bedroom, making yellow smears everywhere. Gary buried his face in the pillows. His sister, Leslie, snatched the diary from among the spilled Cheez Doodles.

"A diary, how do you like that? A diary!" she snarled. "The little sneak. What did she say about me?"

■　□　■

Like Gary Glass among his pillows and Wayne Nolan in the dark, dirty streets, Dezmund O'Herlihy had come to the end of his rope. Jim's girl, Susan, was limping up the stairs after him, dragging her idiotic birds and dressed in her idiotic costume and thanking him continuously for bailing her out of jail, and if she didn't shut up he was going to turn around and fling her bodily down the fire escape.

"Just consider it my final favor, Susan!" he said. "You are sure as hell living up to your reputation!"

"But I'm not . . . I'm not, that's just it, that's just it! I'm not who you think I am!"

"I don't care who you are."

"It's gotten so complicated, I mean it's so crazy, all this. I want to explain. I'm so grateful to you, but I need to explain. . . ."

Dez stopped. He stood poised on the landing. He had locked his door when he left to go to pick up Susan at the jail, and now his door was open.

"Quiet," he said.

"What's the matter?"

"Be quiet. Stay right here."

He stepped carefully toward the door and pushed it open all the way. The lights in his apartment were on. The place had been ransacked. Dozens of reels of film had been unwound and spilled on the floor in a huge, ugly tangle. Dez felt as though somebody had taken his guts out and spilled them.

"Oh my God . . ." murmured Jim's girl, Susan.

"I don't believe it," Dez said. "I don't believe Victoria would do this. . . ." He picked up a piece of the film. He held it to the light. It was his only footage of an East River garbage barge floating downstream at sunrise, a thing of beauty unspooled and trampled.

"Maybe it was the guy who grabbed me last night," whimpered Susan.

"Who?"

"See, he was after me, Dez. Well, not me exactly, he was after Susan, wherever she is, but I'm not her.

And he thinks she's staying here, which she isn't, because I am, see? And I . . ."

"And I don't want to hear it, you got that, Susan? I don't want to hear another word of your phony-baloney bullshit. First I get thrown out of Gunny's on my ass on the sidewalk, then I have to fork up two hundred dollars bail to get you out of jail, now I come home and the whole place is torn apart, why I don't know, and I tell you, I really don't need this shit, Susan, I really do not."

Her incredibly dirty face scrunched up into a tough, resolute pout.

"Fine!" she yelled. "I'll leave!"

She limped huffily over to the mattress and gathered up her stuff, which had been spread all across the floor like Mop & Glo, and she stuffed it into her Dry Bones drum case, and then she tripped on a pillow and her tutu went flying over her head and all the stuff fell out of the drum case, so she gathered it up again, muttering like a bag lady, "You know, I could have been killed last night, Dez. I was really scared! But what do you care? It's all just more phony-baloney bullshit to you! So forget it! And I am very sorry about this mess! If you have incurred any expenses, just send me a bill and I'll give you a check!"

"Great," he said, crouching miserably over his muddled puddle of film. "Another check."

Jim's girl, Susan, got all the stuff back in the drum case and sat on it and pushed with all her strength so it would close and then limped angrily toward the door, determined to make a dignified exit. But then the drum case opened and everything fell out again. She fell to her knees and gathered it all together.

"Sorry," she huffed and puffed, "sorry . . ." and then she began to cry.

Dez sighed. He figured he'd better help her. It looked as though she wasn't ever going to get out of his apartment if he didn't help her. She looked such a wreck, with her stage makeup all smeared like that and her shiny hair tumbled every which way. . . .

"Hey, hey, hey, come on," he said gently, "come on, this mess isn't so bad. I've had worse parties than this."

He crouched next to her, holding the crazy black lace merry-widow bra, and she looked up into his face, and he had to laugh, and she began to laugh, too. And he didn't mean to, he really had never meant to, but he forgot his film spilled on the floor and his $200 lost; he even forgot his good friend Jimmy Riddle, and when he kissed her this time, neither of them made any apologies. She rolled into his arms, and he carried her to the mattress and laid her down like a plate of cookies. Her crazy clothes melted off her. He felt like a virgin, as if she were the first woman who had ever touched him, her hands and her mouth and her legs pulled him into her so deep he felt he could touch her heart. He fell asleep, and she woke him with her touch and rolled over on top of him, and in a couple of minutes he was strong again. The dawn light made her glow. She was the queen of the night and now the angel of the morning, and, for better or worse, she was no longer Jim's girl, Susan.

"Dez, listen to me," she said a little later; she was lying across him, supporting herself on her elbows, her pretty pink nipples grazing his belly. "I'm not Susan. I'm a housewife and I live in Fort Lee, New

Jersey. I've been married four years. My husband, Gary, sells bathroom spas and saunas."

Dez pulled her closer, enjoying the feel of her tits.

"You never stop, do you?" He laughed.

"No, really, really!"

"That's what I like about you. I never know what you're gonna say next. Come here."

He pulled her up by her butt so he could kiss her. Dez did not ordinarily think of himself as one of your all-time great lovers, but something about Susan gave him a lot of extra energy he hadn't known he possessed.

"Oooh, Dez . . ." she whispered, "Dez . . . wait a minute. . . . Listen . . . what is that?"

There were sounds at the front door, light knockings and scrapings.

Dez listened. Roberta listened.

"I don't know," Dez said. "Sounds like somebody's trying to get in."

Dez stood up and wrapped a blanket around himself. From the littered floor, he picked up a film can that was still full and very, very heavy. It might be the blond guy from the Battery; it might be whoever had tried to grab his Susan last night, or whoever had ransacked his apartment. Whoever it was, this intruder was destined to meet with a crashing blow from a calm and steady can.

The man came through the door in the dark. Dez let him have it. He fell, unconscious. Dez bent down and looked at his face. Susan bent down and looked at his face.

"Who is it?" she asked.

"Oh my God," Dez moaned softly. "It's Jim."

t was Susan who selected the Magic Club as the central meeting place for all those desperately seeking something or someone on that final, fateful Saturday night.

Crashing Gary's convertible into the bumper of a more nondescript vehicle (it was Inspector Eugene Licker's undercover spy car, but who knew?), she ignored the parking meter and bopped up the front steps of the New York *Mirror* just ten minutes before the 9:00 A.M. closing deadline for personal-ad insertions.

This was the ad Susan placed in the *Mirror:*

Desperately seeking stranger seeking Susan regarding key. Meet me Saturday night. Magic Club. Broadway, 9:30 P.M. Be there.

"Is that it?" said the clerk. His name was Ovid. He wore a big bow tie. He had seen everything.

"She'll love it," Susan said.

"Pay the cashier."

Along came Blackie. The beautiful redhead in the green jumpsuit had rejected him; just because she loved dogs, it did not follow that she also loved chains and whips. So Blackie had decided to go straight.

"Single white male, 40," he said to the clerk, "looking for afternoon playmates."

"Is that it?" asked Ovid.

"This one had better work or I'm suing your paper, nerd," said Blackie.

"Pay the cashier."

Jimmy Riddle saw the ad first, at a newsstand on West Fifty-seventh Street. He had spent most of the day at the Tea Room hiring Dry Bones a new public-relations firm. This firm promised to get the group mentioned on Page Six at least once a week for the next three months and to instill many articles about Jimmy into hot rock magazines.

Jimmy's social life (as well as Mitzi's and all the other Bones') had been laid out like a chess strategy. Jimmy would be seen with an actress whose perfect body had sold oceans of diet soft drinks. He would be rumored to have moved in with a Pulitzer Prize–winning novelist, famous for her sexual insatiability. It was all cynical bullshit, and Jimmy had resisted commissioning it for his group these many years. But finding out about Susan and Dez so early this morning had suddenly raised Jimmy's cynical-bullshit threshold to new highs. He would show Susan, he should show her, the heartless Pop-Tart. *He would show her!*

If only he could find her.

Jimmy took a cab downtown. He rolled up the *Mirror* into a tight tube and threw it like a javelin onto Dez O'Herlihy's roof, where Dez was relaxing in his hammock, patting Cat, and wondering if he would ever see Susan again.

"Take a look at this, buddy!" yelled Jimmy. "It looks like she's jerking us both around!"

Dez sighed. The delirium of his dawn with Susan had turned into a black depression today. The new Stranger ad just complicated matters more. In his mind, Dez went over the mess again and again, trying to understand what had happened to him.

First of all, there was the shock of seeing Jimmy laid out by the heavy film can. Dez lived through a moment of terror then, because he had not been at all sure that Jimmy would ever wake up. After all, Jimmy was not your most massive guy. And his gig in Buffalo had left him drawn and thin. Dez had patted his face, mopped his brow with a wet cloth, prayed (Please, oh Lord, please let me not have murdered my friend Jimmy Riddle, please. . . .) Then Jimmy opened his eyes.

"Thank God," Dez said. "You had me worried. How you doing?"

"Somebody jumped me," Jimmy said. "It was dark."

"It was me."

Jimmy sat up, holding the back of his head and wincing.

"You?"

"I thought you were somebody else."

"Who did you think I was?"

"Somebody's been following Susan," Dez said. "I thought you were him."

Jimmy blinked his eyes a few times to get his head clear. In the kitchen, Dez could hear the kettle whistling—probably Susan making everybody a cup of coffee. Jimmy took in that Dez was not wearing any clothes. He took in that Dez smelled very good for Dez and looked around, expecting to find some perfumed broad in bed. Nothing but tumultuous blankets in the bed. Jimmy concluded that the broad must be in the kitchen making coffee.

"So who's following Susan?" he asked.

"I can't find out," Dez said. "You know Susan. It's really hard to get a straight answer from her."

Jimmy took in that he was not getting a straight answer from Dez, but he put that thought from his aching head, and said the truth of his heart to Dez, as he was used to doing.

"She needs me, Dez."

"Susan?"

"Yeah, I'm sure of it. She needs me. She's the kind of crazy girl who never wants to make a commitment because it's not her style, and it hurts her ego, but, deep down, I know that when she goes to sleep at night she dreams about me, and when she thinks about her future I'm in it. I'm sure she's just about ready to settle down."

Dez sat back on his haunches and laughed. "Settle down? Susan? Aw come on, Jim, she'd never do that. She's really not the type."

Jimmy took in that Dez was not looking at him.

"Since when do you know her so well?"

Why wasn't Dez looking at him?

"I just can't see her settling down, that's all. I mean she's too wild, but of course that's what is so great about her."

"You really seem to have examined this subject," Jimmy Riddle whispered. Very gently he touched the shoulder of his friend. The jig was up. Dez had to look him straight in the face and tell him.

"Uh . . . we've been . . . um . . . spending some time together. . . . Okay, I'm not gonna bullshit you, Jimmy. It was a shitty thing to do, I'm not saying it wasn't. But you yourself told me she was irresistible."

Jimmy Riddle laughed. He stood up. He stretched himself. He kept on laughing and laughing, very softly. "Oh man, why wh-wh-why don't you just hit me again and finish me off?" He walked across the room to the mattress and kicked it very gently, again and again and again.

"Look now, it's nothing to get hysterical about," Dez insisted. "I mean, it happens, right? The fact is, I'm really crazy about Susan and she's really crazy about me."

Jimmy picked up one of the pillows and threw it at Dez. It was just a pillow, but it really hurt.

"Whatever she told you doesn't mean shit, man!" he yelled. "She plays with people. I mean, I ought to know. I've been chasing her for years!"

"Well, I don't think she's playing with me!" Dez yelled.

"Bullshit!"

Dez pulled on his pants. "Okay," he muttered, "why don't we just ask her? Susan! Susan, get on out here. Susan!"

She was gone. The kettle on the stove still whistled,

but the kitchen window was open and Susan was gone.

"She was right here!" Dez protested. "I swear to God, she was right here."

Jimmy Riddle laughed again, his soft laugh like poison.

Now he had thrown Dez the afternoon New York *Mirror,* with further evidence of the bitter trick that Susan had played on them both, and Dez held his breath, held his nose, stopped breathing for a couple of seconds to control his guilt and shame and anger. He crawled out of his hammock and leaned over the roof edge to see Jimmy.

"You and I are gonna have to go to the Magic Club tonight, buddy," Dez said calmly. "We are gonna have to find Susan and find this stranger and see what gives, because I am very tired of these catastrophic broads, and I no longer wish to think of myself as a schmuck."

■　□　■

Several blocks away, in a Sweete Shoppe drinking his malted milk, Wayne Nolan also read the afternoon papers. He had been cut off from his organization, rendered homeless except for his nondescript car. He felt tired and dirty and downhearted from his fruitless attempts to find the Nefertiti earrings in Roberta's shopping bag or in any can of film in Dez O'Herlihy's apartment.

Wayne thought of abandoning his pursuit of the earrings.

But then he saw that Bruce's girl, Susan, was get-

ting messages again in her usual way, through The
Personals. Nine-thirty, the ad said. The Magic Club.

Wayne figured he should be there.

■   □   ■

Roberta sat on a park bench halfway between
Dez's house and Wayne's Sweete Shoppe.
She felt very bad. How could she, a decent,
well-meaning person, formerly shy and repressed, have broken the hearts of two such wonderful men as Jimmy and Dez in a single night?

They were friends. They had worked together, inspired each other, made things of beauty with each
other's help, and now she had destroyed their friendship, turned them against each other. Oh, it was horrible to think of. It made her faint with guilt.

When she had climbed out the window of Dez's
apartment in a panic, she had meant to go home.

That was hours ago, and she still hadn't gone
home.

How could she return to that awful white, white,
white high-tech kitchen? How could she face a whole
drawer full of pot lids? How could she go back to her
house when some other woman—probably Becky
Shuman, the casting director with the hard hair—
had already moved in and Gary Glass (whom Roberta
had always considered the straightest person in Fort
Lee) was already drunk or high or whatever and giggling maniacally at all hours of the morning.

And anyway, who cared?

Wasn't Gary entitled to some lunacy? Maybe Becky
Shuman wasn't very interested in sex. Maybe Leslie

was right and all Becky wanted was Gary's money and they would be very happy together. Now, should a decent, well-meaning person like Roberta stand in the way of that? Certainly not.

So Roberta did not go home.

On the bench next to her, a real derelict—not a dummy like the one lying outside the Magic Club, who had been left there years before by a panic-stricken ventriloquist in fear of losing his identity—snored under his New York *Mirror*. Roberta glanced at him fondly. His stinking breath blew the newspaper upward in soft peaks, like the egg whites she had so recently used to beat. He looked comfortable and at home on the Lower East Side, just as Roberta now felt. Gently, she reached for the newspaper.

There they were. The Personals.

How dull they seemed now compared to days gone by!

Blackie no longer begged the girl in the green jumpsuit to requite his love; the seventh-grade teacher had obviously found her hunk and the lonely widower his tender, patient dreamgirl, the lascivious Shirl no longer cried out to Harry to bring *it* back home. Now only straightforward demands for plain old sex appeared. *Single white male, 40, wants* . . . It was so uninspiring!

And then she saw the ad that was meant for her.

Desperately seeking stranger . . . it said.

That's me! Roberta thought. She's found me! Susan has found me! She's a genius!

"Come on, little birdies," she said to her doves and her duck, "we're gonna go home to the Magic Club

and practice, and tonight we're gonna give our friend
Susan the show of her life!"

■   □   ■

Something mean and tense surges through the
thick air of the Magic Club tonight," mused
Kaminsky the dummy. "Have you noticed?"
Wonder Woman and Claudette Colbert
pulled their capes tighter around their shoulders and
shivered, because Kaminsky was right. The sleepy
club seemed to seethe with unprecedented tension.

First of all, word of Ian the magician's charming
new assistant had spread through the neighborhood
all day, bringing in new customers, *lots* of customers,
young customers.

They ordered unmixed drinks.

They constantly used the toilet.

They talked so loudly they woke up the waitresses.

Quick, quick, Gilda called around and found a couple of extra bartenders.

Ray told a new joke. "Anybody here from
Queens?" he asked the packed house. A few customers said yes. "Too bad," Ray said. "I'm from normal
parents myself."

The band played two, maybe three, chords at once.
But the crowd booed. They didn't want to hear Ray's
dumb jokes. They wanted to see Davina, Queen of
the Night.

Feeling that an agent might be out there, or a rich
PTA president, Ian the magician paced back and
forth backstage and rapped nervously on the door of
the ladies' dressing room. "Don't be late, Susan," he

whispered. "Tonight's the night. Tonight is special. Tonight could be the beginning of something *big!*"

Susan made her grand entrance in a new black sequined jacket and clean clothes. She also apparently had a new boyfriend. "Very different from Susan's wont," Gilda commented, looking over Gary Glass. What a cool customer he was! Comfortable, charming, obviously accustomed to slumming in dives like the Magic Club, he chatted with the Eurasian mannequin, he lit the cigarettes of an older gentleman with blond braids, and he admired the pink hair of a punk couple who had brought their pet sea elephant.

"I love a man who can get along anywhere," said Wonder Woman.

"Who's the laid-back guy with the disheveled black curls and the long, clean fingers?" whispered Claudette Colbert lustfully.

"And who is that magnificent creature on his arm?" cried Kaminsky. "Now *that's* what I call a real woman! During my youth in the once-happy city of Minsk, we used to have women like that. The same glittering teeth, the same flashy jewels, the same frenzied tension, only fatter!"

Little did Kaminsky realize that the source of Leslie's tension was her fury with her pig brother, Gary, whom she would never, but never, forgive for dragging her and Larry along on this disgusting foray into the netherworld. To Susan, she would not speak altogether. As far as Leslie was concerned, Susan was one of those people who got themselves remembered in the wills of other women's husbands and had to be guarded against constantly, like nuclear proliferation. She hated it that Susan was stroking Gary's shoulder with her black fingernails and whispering in Gary's ear and drawing the attention of every man in the Magic Club as she left their table and bopped away.

"What did she say to you?" Leslie hissed.

"She said we're in for a real surprise," Gary answered.

"Well, I guess we're not gonna see Tony Bennett in this place," offered Larry.

"I'd settle for a police escort," Leslie growled. "How could you let her wear that fabulous jacket I bought for Roberta at Osterfein's, Gary?"

"Hey, she's cold. Roberta took her jacket! She's got to wear something!"

Larry Stillman watched Susan as she wiggled her ass past the guys at the bar. "God, she's gorgeous," he said.

"Beauty fades," Leslie purred. One day Larry Stillman would pay for that.

Dez O'Herlihy and Jimmy Riddle circled around the periphery of the club, dressed in black, like panthers, and just as jumpy. With restless eyes they searched for Susan. Jim absently bumped into Wayne Nolan's table, jostling Wayne's third brandy. "I wouldn't make me nervous tonight if I were you, minibrain," mumbled Wayne dangerously, but Jimmy didn't hear him; Jimmy just moved on.

"If she sees us both here, she'll probably just split again," Jim commented.

"You could go home," Dez commented.

"I want to see who this stinking stranger is," Jim said to himself.

A flash of glitter, a drum roll, a chord!

"There she is! Susan!"

Dez didn't see her.

"Over there, talking to the cigarette girl!" Jimmy yelled.

"That's not Susan," Dez said.

"That's Susan! Don't you think I should know?"

"Well, that might be *a* Susan," Dez insisted, "but it's not *my* Susan, and if that's *your* Susan, then who was the girl at the Battery?"

Jim followed Susan to the ladies' room. He saw her rhinestone-studded boots under the stall door. She flushed the toilet and came out, and when she saw him, she threw her arms around his neck and laughed. "Jimmy! You're home!"

"Who's the stranger?"

"How was Buffalo?"

"Take your hands out of my pants, Susan. Who's the stranger?"

Susan grinned. "You wouldn't know her," she said softly. She loved the look of relief on his face, she just loved it. She pulled him close. She bit his tongue and licked the roof of his mouth. *"Her?"* he said between kisses. *"Her? Her?* You . . . you . . ."

"Come on," Susan said. "Let's go talk about it in private."

Back at the bar, Dez O'Herlihy paid for his drink and got ready to give up and go home. Then he saw a flash of glitter! A drum roll! A chord! There she was, *his* Susan!

Cool and practiced, she pranced across the stage with her cooing caged birds, right in the rhythm of the Strauss waltzes, while Ian the magician waved his cape and produced magic fires. God, she was beautiful. Even in that crazy new black-lace tutu she was wearing and those crazy black net gloves and that incredible wig with the single huge earring dangling from it, she was the most beautiful woman in New York, and what was more, she could *act!* A great talent! Dez thought. Stardom in her future! Look how deftly she manages those fluttering doves! Look how gracefully she plucks the duck from the platter!

At a table nearby, Dez was shocked to see a balding guy in a three-piece suit leap to his feet. Was it possible that anybody could wish to leave in the middle of such a sensational magic act? The growling woman next to the man grabbed him by the seat of his pants and said "Sit down, Gary!" And the other guy they were with had the good sense to applaud enthusiastically, smacking this fool Gary on the back and saying, "You know, she's really good, Gary. She's got real style in a way, sort of. . . ."

Suddenly a hush fell over the Magic Club. Ian the magician was about to perform his great pièce de résistance, the unbelievable, incredible, astounding Lady-in-the-Coffin trick!

Smiling coquettishly, Dez's girl, Susan, stepped into the terrifying Transylvanian black wood coffin. She eased onto her back, wiggling her body. Because the side of the coffin was flipped down, the audience could see that she was all in one piece in there, and what a piece she was!

Cackling savagely, Ian crept around the side of the coffin and closed the open panel. Now all the audience could see was Susan's blonde head with its dangling big gold earring and her feet in their black lace stockings. An evil gleam entered Ian's eyes. But his beautiful assistant kept smiling, winking at the audience, blowing little kisses to a guy who looked like Burt Reynolds (sort of).

Ian picked up a long, gleaming saw. Drum roll. He held it aloft so the lights flashed on it. Drum roll. He flexed it and felt its blade with his pinky finger and just to authenticate its razor sharpness, he *cut* his pinky finger and displayed a drop of scarlet blood.

The audience gasped. Dez's girl, Susan, went "Oooh." Dez ordered another scotch. His Susan was no longer laughing and winking and blowing kisses; her large eyes rolled toward the audience, full of terror. The patrons stopped breathing, their hearts beating madly, their drinks clinking in their trembling hands.

Ian began to saw. Drum roll. Ian kept sawing. The drum kept rolling. Wayne Nolan finished his brandy and started his fifth. Ian kept sawing. Gary Glass wiped the sweat off his face. Ian kept sawing.

Suddenly the beautiful lady in the coffin screamed. Leslie Glass screamed and knocked her whole rum and Tab onto Larry Stillman's lap, ice and all, but Larry Stillman didn't move. He couldn't take his eyes off the screaming lady in the coffin. Wayne kept drinking. Ian kept sawing. The lady kept screaming. Gary kept sweating. Ian sawed through the entire width of the box, and gritting his teeth, groaning with the strain, he p-p-pulled the two halves of the box apart.

The head of the lady stopped screaming and began to giggle. Her feet in the other end of the bisected box began to wiggle. Ian stood majestically between the two severed halves of his assistant and took his bow. The audience went crazy.

People leaped onto tables, cheering and applauding. An outpouring of swizzle sticks and maraschino cherries flew approvingly onto the stage. The band played chord after chord and Ian took bow after bow and Dez yelled, "Bravo!"

Gary Glass fell off his chair and collapsed under his table.

Wayne Nolan leaped over Gary's prone body and surged onto the stage and snatched the crazy blonde wig and the gigantic gold earring.

"That's the guy!" Dez's girl, Susan, screamed. "That's him! That's the guy who jumped me in the alley! Help!"

Wayne ran as fast as his lousy feet could carry him, offstage left, plowing into Ray the manager, who was kissing the Eurasian mannequin, plowing into Kaminsky and flinging him up into the fly space with the lights.

"Somebody stop that guy!" screamed Roberta in her coffin. "Help! Help! Stop that man!"

"Lower the curtain!" cried Ian the magician.

"Get me down from here!" cried Kaminsky. (But who heard?)

Ian produced flowers from his pockets, doves from his pants. He took off his shoes and made a magic fire leap between his toes, but nothing could calm the enthusiasm of the awakened patrons of the Magic Club. Dez and Gary ran up on the stage. Gary was trying to find the opening in the curtain. Dez dispensed with that formality and crawled under. Behind the curtain, Roberta was still trapped in her coffin, screaming bloody murder.

"Did that blond guy hurt you?" Gary Glass yelled, clutching her left hand. "I'll kill him. I swear, I'll kill him."

"Gary!" she cried.

"What the hell is going on here?" Dez yelled, clutching her right hand. "Are you okay, Susan?"

"Dez!" she cried.

"Don't worry about it, fella, I can take care of this, I'm in charge from here on in," said Gary Glass.

"Who is this guy?" Dez asked.

"Who am I? Who are *you?*" Gary asked.

Roberta went, *"Aghhhh!"* just to get their attention. "Would you please get me out of this coffin, fellas?"

They obligingly unlocked and unhinged her box, and she gratefully uncoiled, her tutu turned inside out and stuck around her neck like a lobster bib. Gary modestly pulled the tutu down.

"Get your hands off her tutu!" Dez yelled, pushing Gary.

"You get your hands off *me,* you degenerate! Roberta, who is this guy?"

Roberta took a deep breath.

"Gary," she said, "this is Dez. Dez, this is my husband, Gary."

Dez stared at her.

"The hot-tub salesman?"

"That's right, Dez."

"No shit, so you were telling me the truth last night!"

Roberta nodded her tousled head, helpless, quite helpless; however, not crying.

"Last night?" Gary said. "Did you spend the night with this guy? Oh my God . . . wait a minute . . . is he the pimp the police were telling me about?"

"I am not a pimp!" Dez yelled.

"He's not a pimp, Gary!" Roberta yelled.

"I'm a friend of hers!"

Gary Glass squinted at Dezmund O'Herlihy, who appeared to be a normal man in a normal black tweed jacket. He squinted at Roberta, his wife, who appeared to have lost her mind and become a magician's assistant. He really wished his sister, Leslie, would come backstage here and tell him why all this was happening and what he should do now.

"Dez, I really need to talk to Gary alone, okay, Dez?" Roberta said gently.

Dez sighed. "Okay," he said, "I guess that's a good idea, because I, uh, really need some time alone right now, too, Susan. . . ."

Gary helped his wife down from the coffin. He figured she had been without his guidance now for more than forty-eight hours and must need comfort. So he hugged her to him and said, "It's all right, it's all right, the nightmare's over."

■   □   ■

M eanwhile, Wayne Nolan stumbled and staggered through the labyrinthine corridors under the Magic Club, clutching the blonde wig with its precious dangling Nefertiti earring and looking for a way out. Somehow he had gotten caught in another museum! Racks of costumes, stacks of props tripped him and sprayed their dust onto his head, in his eyes. He found a door and threw his whole weight against it, but it would not budge. He shuffled into a dark room and felt for the light, and, when he turned it on, the roaches and mice scurried away into their hat boxes, behind their music stands, under their Shakespearean robes. Wayne turned off the light and doubled back. He heard tinkling bells and soft laughter up ahead someplace, people sounds, and, although he was afraid of people right now, he knew he had to take one of them hostage if he was ever to get out of there alive.

He stubbed his toes on a prone bass-fiddle case and stifled a cry of pain and shuffled on, limping. Through beaded curtains, past yards of musty velour draping, he shuffled, heading toward the sound of the laughter and the tinkling bells. He tore through a ragged scrim and found Jim and Susan making love on a pinball machine.

To Wayne, they were strangers. Very unlucky strangers.

The woman writhed on her back on the machine, her legs locked around her partner, whose pants had fallen to the floor around his ankles. They didn't see Wayne or feel his presence; they were too engrossed with each other. Nor did Susan hear the telltale squeaking of his orthopedic shoes.

In perfect silence, Wayne pressed his gun to Susan's temple and dragged her away from her lover. "Don't make a peep," Wayne whispered to the terrified girl. "You're gonna be my ticket out of here." He locked his free arm tightly around her neck. She gagged and gasped, but she did not scream. Wayne looked right into Jim's uncomprehending eyes. "Not one peep." He pointed the stubby black gun at Susan's wet cheek, at her soft, white neck, at her dark blue eyes, and hauled her with him down the corridor. He pushed her through a room stacked high with old furniture, keeping the gun firmly at the base of her skull. She felt its ice-cold message. She stayed silent.

Wayne saw a stairway. "Up," he whispered. "Up to the roof."

Susan let him push her up the stairs; the skylight at the top was locked. "You can't get through," she gasped. But, to her horror, Bruce Meeker's ex-partner put the wig in his mouth and kept the gun to her head and with one hand tenderly stroked and manipulated the lock until the skylight flew open. Then he pushed her out onto the roof.

She gulped the night air and started to scream. He clapped his hand over her mouth and her nose. She couldn't breathe.

Below them, patrons of the Magic Club ran, hunting the thug who had stolen the wig of Davina, Queen of the Night. Wayne pinned Susan's legs; he pinned her arms; he gagged her with the wig; she couldn't move, she felt as though she were being killed. Her potential rescuers passed mindlessly below, never thinking to look up the dusty staircase.

Below her, in the ladies' dressing room, Gary Glass patted his pretty wife, mumbling about nightmares, but only Susan was having one. She had to get away. She had to run and scream and kick. She had to get away or he would kill her the way she thought he had killed Bruce Meeker. With all her strength, she twisted in his iron grasp and freed one elbow and plowed it into his stomach. Wayne grunted and relaxed his grip. For a split second, Susan plunged freely across the roof, but he caught her again and threw her down on the pebbly tar, scratching her face, loosening her hair, rubbing her teeth in the dirt.

Wayne rolled her over and grabbed her ear. "Wait, wait, what is thi—Where'd you get this?" With a mighty yank, he pulled the second Nefertiti earring straight through Susan's ear. A thin trickle of blood ran down onto the shoulder of her sequined jacket. Susan sobbed. His hand came down on her mouth like a lead weight. "Stay," he said. He held the earring up to the light of the moon and examined it, holding his gun right at the juncture of her jaw and neck, where the first bullet to leave that gun had entered the body of Bruce Meeker.

Susan looked at the sky above New York, looked at the stars and prayed, prayed that one, just one, would be lucky for her and save her from dying on this filthy rooftop.

In the ladies' dressing room right underneath Wayne and Susan, Gary Glass decided to stop patting Roberta and get tough.

"All right," he said. "Now. I want some answers. What are you doing in this place?"

"This is where I work," she said.

"Why did you leave me?"

"It was an accident."

"An accident? An accident? And when you were out soliciting in the streets, I suppose that was an accident, too, right?"

Roberta looked at herself in the mirror above the dressing table. She knew she had to have courage. She knew she was not crazy or frigid, that there was nothing wrong with her body, that she did not need braces. She had to have courage; she had to be patient and tender and try to make Gary Glass see the truth.

"It all started with The Personals," she explained. "There was this ad in The Personals . . . *Desperately seeking Susan* . . ." She stopped. She realized that, as always, Gary was paying no attention to her.

"Why were you in jail?" he asked. "Do you realize that everybody in Fort Lee, every salesman at Gary's Oasis, every customer, the beauty-parlor guy and the dry-cleaning guy, they all think you left me and . . . Just tell the truth, Roberta. Why were you in jail?"

"The police thought I was a prostitute, so they arrested me, but I'm not. It was a mistake. I'm not . . ."

"Are you a lesbian, Roberta? Leslie says lots of prostitutes are lesbians." He was fingering the costumes on the rack.

Gary was definitely not listening to her. He was not *seeing* her. It was the same as always, and it would always be the same. "We'll get professional help," he decided. "I don't care how much it costs. The important thing is that I want you to come home with me."

Roberta brought both her fists down hard on the table; all the junk jumped with fear.

"Why?" she yelled. "Why do you want me to come home with you, Gary?"

At this moment, she looked very much like Mommy in court. Gary put that thought from his mind and decided Roberta was on drugs.

"Come on now, don't get excited, just what . . . just tell me what exactly you are hooked on. Now out with it."

Roberta charged at him like a jungle cat, tearing at his vest, popping his buttons. "Look at me, Gary! For once, just once, *look at me!*"

"I looked at you," he said, not looking at her. "You look ridiculous."

"Look at me, Gary. Listen to me. I am not coming home with you!"

The only regret Roberta had when she uttered those final words was that she might not be able to see her sister-in-law, Leslie, again, and of all the people she knew, Leslie would probably have profited most from what Roberta would have to tell her about these last few days of life as Susan.

Besides that, Leslie had been her friend, the only person to receive favorable mention in her diary, the only person to think, really think, about what to give her on her birthday, even though Roberta had not felt exactly grateful at the time. She smiled to herself. She remembered Mom saying (of all the meaningless gifts they had bought in bunches on sale), "It's the thought that counts, my sweet honey angel."

Mom had turned out to be right about a lot of things.

"You are just tired," Gary Glass was saying to her.

"I'm not coming home with you, Gary."

"Get changed and we'll talk about it at home."

"I'm not coming home."

"I'm gonna go outside, and I'm gonna wait for five minutes, Roberta."

"You give my love to Leslie. Tell her I'll call her. We'll have lunch, we'll go shopping."

"If you are not out there in five minutes exactly, I am going to leave without you."

"Goodbye, Gary," she said.

She did not see him as he left. She saw only herself

in the mirror, a sexy woman in a black lace costume, with a good job and a magnificent lover and a future full of fantasies that would probably all come true.

At the very least, Roberta Glass would never, ever be invisible again.

She took a swig from the bottle of liquor Gilda left handy for such occasions and drank a toast to herself.

Suddenly! Through the open window of the dressing room tumbled Susan, bruised and bleeding and filthy, with Wayne Nolan right behind her, pointing a gun at her head.

Susan looked at Roberta, and without making a sound she mouthed the two words she had never even thought before in her entire life: "Help me!"

Roberta picked up the bottle of scotch, and with all her might crashed it down on Wayne Nolan's golden head. He fell to the floor, unconscious. His gun went flying. But the precious Nefertiti earrings stayed locked in his golden hands. (It would turn out that the gun contained no bullets, for Wayne had emptied it after his tragic encounter with Bruce Meeker. This would favorably impress the jury, who would give Wayne a mere five years in the slammer, but would do little to protect him from the wrath of his assorted wives.)

Through the window came Jimmy Riddle in a heap, not a graceful guy when you came right down to it, and now extremely winded from his pursuit of Susan and her crazy kidnapper. He sprawled, stunned, next to the collapsed body of Wayne Nolan.

"What's going on?!" he exclaimed. Susan gave him a kiss.

To Roberta, she offered her hand in what would

prove to be lifelong friendship. "Good going, Stranger," she said, and she winked and laughed her merry laugh.

■　□　■

Susan and Roberta loved returning the Nefertiti earrings to the curator of the Cairo Museum and receiving their half of the $200,000 reward. They got all dressed up in fancy black outfits for the ceremonies at City Hall. The Egyptian ambassador kissed their hands. The mayor gave them the keys to the city.

■　□　■

After the festivities, Roberta found Dez O'Herlihy in his projection booth, projecting.
She had no shame. She had forgotten "shy" and repressed "repressed." She refused to wait for the movie to end, but forced Dez to make love with her right there on the projection-room floor. The film, an outer-space classic that had inspired Spielberg and Asimov, caught fire.

Down below in the theater, the crowd hissed and booed.

But not Susan.

She just laid her weary head on Jimmy Riddle's shoulder and let him feed her popcorn. He told her he loved her, and that was the God's honest truth. She told him her last name.

■　□　■

Do you have an opinion about all this, Mom?" Ted Koppel asked Roberta's mother on "Nightline." "Is this the way women like you *want* their daughters to turn out?"

Mom laughed.

"What the hell," she said, "one generation's mystique is the next generation's material."